THE BOY WHO SPOKE DOG

THE BOY WHO SPOKE DOG

CLAY MORGAN

PUFFIN BOOKS

The spiral designs used to ornament this book were inspired by tattoos and carvings of the Maori people of New Zealand, which they call Aotearoa, "the land of the long white cloud." Spirals and twists hint at surprises and new beginnings.

This book is a work of fiction. Names, characters, places, and incidents are either the product of the author's imagination or are used fictitiously, and any resemblance to actual persons, living or dead, business establishments, events, or locales is entirely coincidental.

PUFFIN BOOKS
Published by the Penguin Group
Penguin Young Readers Group, 345 Hudson Street, New York, New York 10014, U.S.A.
Penguin Group (Canada), 10 Alcorn Avenue, Toronto,
Ontario, Canada M4V 3B2 (a division of Pearson Penguin Canada Inc.)
Penguin Books Ltd, 80 Strand, London WC2R 0RL, England
Penguin Ireland, 25 St Stephen's Green, Dublin 2, Ireland (a division of Penguin Books Ltd)
Penguin Group (Australia), 250 Camberwell Road, Camberwell, Victoria 3124,
Australia (a division of Pearson Australia Group Pty Ltd)
Penguin Books India Pvt Ltd, 11 Community Centre,
Panchsheel Park, New Delhi - 110 017, India
Penguin Group (NZ), Cnr Airborne and Rosedale Roads, Albany, Auckland,
New Zealand (a division of Pearson New Zealand Ltd)
Penguin Books (South Africa) (Pty) Ltd, 24 Sturdee Avenue,
Rosebank, Johannesburg 2196, South Africa

Registered Offices: Penguin Books Ltd, 80 Strand, London WC2R 0RL, England

First published in the United States of America by Dutton Children's Books,
a division of Penguin Young Readers Group, 2003
Published by Puffin Books, a division of Penguin Young Readers Group, 2005

10

Copyright © Clay Morgan, 2003
All rights reserved
CIP Data is available.
Designed by Richard Amari
ISBN 978-0-14-240343-3

Printed in the United States of America

This book is dedicated to the dog in all of us.

There were reports, long ago, of a castaway boy who had survived among wild dogs on one of the islands. It was claimed that this boy had learned to speak with the dogs. He understood them. He thought like them. He became part dog himself. Many sailors and New Zealanders doubted the stories, but the tales endured of the boy who spoke dog....

I

Hold on, Moxie!" Kelso barked. "Ride him longer. Ride him and then jump to another sheep. Hold on! Ride him! Ready? Jump!"

But Moxie could not jump. She was out in the middle of the flock, a little dog riding a powerful ram. She dug her paws into the shaggy wool near the ram's neck. She felt jump-ready and able, and yet something was stopping her. It was a new odor in the air. Moxie lowered her head. She smelled the ram's rank lanolin, but that wasn't it. This ram smelled slightly mean and somewhat stupid. So Moxie got ready again to jump. She got ready, and she got ready, but she could not make herself jump.

"Jump!" Kelso barked, and Moxie thought, *Jump!* Her

shoulders quivered, but she could not jump. What was it? She could smell everything, and her nose kept her aware. She smelled, at this moment, that it was summer on the island. It was just after sunset. The breezes were changing from sea salt to meadow grass. The dogs and the sheep were in the island's great meadow near the burnt ruins on top of the seacliff, high above the ocean. The sky was darkening past blue to gray. Moxie smelled the colors better than she could see them. She smelled other things, too, at the moment invisible. From the dark of the nearby forest, Moxie smelled the dread and wild fangos. The fango smell chilled her, but that wasn't it, either. The fangos were always there, waiting and watching.

"Jump, Moxie!" Kelso yipped. He was growing impatient.

OK, then. I'll jump, Moxie thought. She crouched. She tensed. She almost jumped. But then—what? Moxie now recognized the scent. It was a lightning smell—summer lightning, sharp and prickling. No clouds hovered above, but nearby from the mainland, a thunderous storm was approaching. As Moxie rode the big ram, she read the air with her nose. She looked to Kelso, the sheep dogs' leader. The big German shepherd held his nose to the sky, too. Kelso had smelled the lightning.

Moxie now picked up another scent—the smell of fear in

the sheep. It smelled tallowy and thick and generally stupid. And the sheep fear smell rose out of the flock, and it curdled into the storm's lightning smell. Together, they set off an alarm in Moxie's brain—now she really *had* to jump.

But before she could, there came a low, boulder-rolling rumble of thunder. Now Moxie more than smelled the fear and lightning in the air. She felt the fear moving up through the ram she was riding. The ram's fear quivered up through her legs, and it shook her. Moxie glanced back at Kelso for help, but Kelso had turned away.

Kelso was barking to all the sheep dogs, "Vigilance! Vigilance! Huddle up the flock!"

The older dogs got to work. They began rounding the sheep into a bumping froth of butting, bleating woollies. Moxie struggled to stay on top of her ram in the middle of the flock. She barely kept her balance, and then the ram began to buck. Moxie teetered. She lost her footing. She fell off the ram and tumbled into the sheep. Suddenly she was lost in a swarm of thin, black kicking legs.

As the sheep milled and bleated, Moxie was knocked down and knocked over and batted between the hammering hooves. She dodged and darted, but she got kicked in the head and she fell. She scrambled up. She fell again. She looked for an opening. A scrap of dull daylight appeared right above her, and Moxie was able to clamber up onto an old ewe. Moxie balanced there for a moment, in the ewe's thick, wobbly fleece. Then she jumped to another sheep's back—then to another and another—until she had jumped her way to the edge of the flock. Moxie fell off the last sheep and tumbled at the feet of Kelso.

She had made it! She looked up at Kelso for praise. But he was still distracted. It was the storm. Now it hit. First came a hard smell of ocean, then a great crash of light and a big smell of lightning. A ton of thunder fell out of the clouds, and a pummult of rain pounded down on the dogs and their sheep. The sheep panicked. The older dogs worked harder. Kelso barked, "Keep them bunched! Keep them together! Keep them rounded. Be vigilant!"

Then he barked, "Watch for fangos!"

Fangos! That bark rang alarms inside Moxie. She wanted to help, but she got all wound up. She ran in a tight, useless circle that only made her dizzy. The older dogs worked hard along the flock's edges to make the sheep hold. The sheep bleated and bawled, wild-eyed with terror. They bucked at any chance to break out and away.

Then from the near distance, a guard dog barked a new warning. "Fangos! It's the fangos! The fangos are here!"

Here? Moxie's fear sprang open wider. All the dogs

whirled around just as a ragged wave of fangos burst out of the forest. With teeth slashing and eyes flashing in the strobing stabs of lightning, the fangos came streaking across the meadow. They darted and dashed at the edges of the flock. They disappeared and reappeared. The sheep were now frenzied. They bleated. They butted each other's heads. They climbed onto each other's backs. And then they bolted. The sheep burst through the thin defense of sheep dogs, and they ran straight toward the top of the sea-cliff.

Kelso yelped. "Stop them! Get around them! Get in front of the sheep!"

The sheep dogs now became one fighting-and-saving machine. Stop the sheep! Fight the fangos! Guard the puppies! The older dogs turned to fight the fangos. The faster heelers raced ahead of the sheep to keep them from plunging off the sea-cliff. Moxie started to run with the heelers, but she was not fast enough, so she turned to fight with the older dogs. She found herself standing right next to old Sage. Sage may have been blind, but Moxie knew the old English sheepdog was fearless. He presented to the fangos his growling, snarling power. Moxie growled, too, but she was shivering with fear.

The fango front line was surging, right there in front of her. The lightning's scatter made every fango look like four.

Their yellow eyes flared. Their yellow forms jumped. The fangos moved nearer, and their yellow teeth slavered with drool. Moxie clamped her jaws and tried to swallow her fear. The fangos closed in. Blind Sage stepped forward. Moxie wondered how he could fight, and she looked back frantically behind her for help.

Seen through the gray slant of hard rain, the mass of sheep seemed to thicken. Then the whole flock shuddered, and Moxie saw the sheeps' heads all turn. She saw Kelso and the other sheep dogs come charging toward her, leaping across the backs of the sheep that they had turned away from the sea-cliff.

Suddenly Kelso stood beside Moxie. The hair on his shoulders swelled and made him look titanically strong. Another snarling sheep dog stood on Sage's other side. And another stood her ground beyond him. The great storm blasted and crashed and thundered, and the fangos threatened, but the brave and loyal sheep dogs never backed down. Shoulder to shoulder, they braced each other and faced down the fangos. Moxie stood with the older dogs and watched the fangos slink away, but her fear was slower to leave. She stood, still quivering in wonder at her fear, and she realized the storm, too, had passed. It had already crossed the sheep dogs' island and was heading out over the ocean.

2

Just offshore from the island, the storm was now about to hit an old Baltimore schooner as the ship was nearing the sea-cliffs. She was named the *Patty B*. She was out of San Francisco. She carried a large cargo of New Zealand wool and a short crew of salty, brave sailors. She also carried a cabin boy named Jack, who had lost his parents in the big San Francisco earthquake.

Jack was below decks in the galley, paring potatoes and helping old Cookie with a supper of potato scouse. The oil lamps swung gently in their gimbals. The sailors of the next watch slept and swung creaking in their hammocks.

"Mmm, now. Slice 'em smaller, Jackie Tar," Cookie directed. "We may be eating these raw. In a storm, perhaps?"

Jack hoped that Cookie was joking. He looked over to see the old man first grin and then frown—and then scowl and then nod. Oh, what a sight this Nantucket man was! Cookie could look happy and angry and sleepy all at once.

Or he could sleep with his eyes open, so that Jack thought he was awake. At those times, as Jack would slowly realize Cookie was asleep, Cookie would start talking. In his sleep, he told stories. Big stories. And long ones. The sailors gathered around him and listened. It was the strangest, finest thing to watch and be a part of. Cookie was like a book full of stories and a story in himself. Jack loved him for it, and so did the sailors.

And when Cookie awoke and he stood, the treats were not over. "I've had the strangest dream!" he said. And then he told the same story, all over again, only better.

Cookie was short and squat, with a mad, merry face and a bald, shiny head. He had one long, furry white eyebrow, which crawled like a caterpillar over his eyes. He had only three teeth—two on the top and one on the bottom. As he chewed, his teeth made his pipe jump and jitter. His sweet Virginia pipe smoke wound around him and around Jack, in looping coils and knots.

"Mmm—yes!" he said now, sitting beside Jack. "Eat 'em taters raw! With salt! Will Captain like that?"

The old sailor's pipe was jumping, a-jitter. Then Cookie did something that only he could do. First he blew a smoke ring. Then he stuck his finger into his mouth. Then he poked his finger into the smoke ring and twirled it around, causing the smoke to spool around his finger. Then he pulled his finger out, leaving a perfect blue, spinning spiral.

Jack asked him again how he did that.

"Sticky smoke," Cookie said. "You need a wet finger."

"Sticky smoke?" Jack asked.

But Cookie held up his hand. He said, "What now? Does the captain—?" He looked behind, toward the hatch.

"What—?" Jack began.

Cookie looked back at Jack. He held his finger to his lips. Then his eyebrow slowly arched. His eyes opened wide.

"What!" he said. "What now? Now trouble?"

"What?" Jack said, and he looked all around. He sensed nothing, but around him the sailors began to squirm in their hammocks. They sensed something, too.

"Oh, now! Feel it?" Cookie whispered hoarsely. Jack felt nothing. Then Cookie's pipe dropped from his mouth. "HERE SHE COMES!" he shouted.

And the whole world lurched as a great wave struck the ship. The kettle rolled over. Potatoes bounced and flew. Jack grabbed hold of the table to keep from following after them.

A great roar of storm filled the hold. Jack looked to Cookie for assurance. Cookie already had his pipe back and in his mouth. Cookie clamped down on it in a way that made Jack laugh.

"No. No," Cookie said. "This is not a laugh." He looked upward toward the deck and held up his finger. "It is bad. Hark!"

Jack heard it now, from topside, a faint voice above the roar. "All—hands—! Ahoy—!"

The ship yawed and heaved. All hands! Around Jack, the hammocks began squirming and dropping their sailors. The men fell out and scrambled into their shoes and shirts. The big Maori twins—Toa and Tanati—were the first to head topside. They were Jack's favorites. They passed shoeless and shirtless, their chests and faces so completely tattooed that they looked like they wore costumes and masks.

"Jackie Tar!" Toa shouted to Jack as he ran past. Tanati flashed Jack a pointy grin of filed teeth.

"Toa! Tanati!" Jack yelled. This was big excitement. "All hands!" Jack shouted at Cookie. But Cookie pointed his finger at Jack, to stay him where he was.

"Not you, yet," said Cookie. "No. Not yet you." Cookie shook his finger. "Me. I go."

Cookie jammed his pipe into a pocket and hurried after

the last sailor. He climbed through the hatch but stopped to look back at Jack. Cookie opened his mouth to speak, but a heavy wave banged the hatch shut with a splash. Around Jack, all the lamps blew out.

Jack was alone in the dark, among the empty, swinging hammocks. The ship rolled and pitched. Now Jack heard the thunder. It roared as the *Patty B* pitched on the sea.

Outside the wind howled. Jack could not stand to hear it alone. He staggered to the hatch and pushed it up so he could look out. Hard spray stung his eyes. He squinted and blinked. He saw nothing. Then lightning flashed. In the scattering dazzle, Jack saw sailors wrestling with the riggings and Captain Day clinging to the wheel.

Jack was about to join them, but another great wave struck the ship. It slammed the hatch shut and knocked him back onto the table. Jack rolled over it and onto the floor. He stood again, staggering. He started toward the hatch, but the ship began to roll.

In the din and in the dark, what happened next felt unreal. The ship seemed to lift first and then tip, and then it kept rolling. Jack tumbled back against the table. He grabbed on to it and held tightly, grateful that it was bolted to the floor. A second later, the entire ship keeled over, topside down.

"Aaaahh—! Aaaahh—!" Jack yelled as he hung from the table. Two great booms shook the hull and resounded in Jack's ears. Then the *Patty B* rolled back upright. All her timbers shivered, and she started to spin.

Jack crawled blindly to the hatch. With great effort he lifted it, but outside he saw nothing but the storm.

Then the lightning blazed blue off the black deck. Jack saw only empty decking and the spinning ship's wheel. The ship's masts were gone, as were the riggings and the quarter boat. And all of the men? Had they been washed overboard?

But in another flash, Jack saw Captain Day stand up from behind the wheel. The captain grabbed the wheel, and with great effort he stopped its spinning. Then two figures emerged into view. Jack recognized Toa first, staggering but strong. Then Tanati reemerged into the blinking scene. Great Tanati lugged what looked like a heavy sack, which Jack quickly realized was Cookie.

Jack felt cheered, but the feeling didn't last. None of the other sailors appeared from the storm. Jack realized that they were the only ones left—the captain, Toa, Tanati, Cookie, and himself. A sick fear overwhelmed him. He let the hatch shut, and he crawled back into the dark to lie down beneath the table.

But not for long. Within minutes, he felt great hands grab his shoulders.

"Come, Jackie Tar! We save you," Tanati said.

"What?" Jack said weakly.

"You come, Jack," Tanati said. He lifted Jack and carried him outside onto the deck. He hauled Jack in front of Captain Day. The captain held the wheel steady, although the ship was still spinning in the storm.

The captain was shouting at Cookie. "We may be sunk! But I want to chance it! And I don't want to chance young Jack!"

Now they both looked at Jack, and Cookie nodded.

"You'll float!" the captain shouted at Jack. "You'll have a better hope on a raft!"

"What?" Jack said. He looked back to Cookie. Cookie seemed both furious and forlorn.

"Hope, Jack! Hope!" Cookie shouted.

Then Tanati turned Jack around, and Jack saw Toa with a bale of sheep's wool. A rope had been tied around its middle. Tanati jammed Jack onto the bale, pressing Jack's face against its stamped brand, *Roratua Ranch*. Toa looped the rope's free end twice around Jack's wrist; then he closed Jack's hand around the rope's tail.

"You sabbee, Jack! Sabbee?" Toa shouted into his ear. "You hold on! No swim! You float."

"Jack float!" Toa shouted at his twin brother. "Him float! Him sabbee?" The Maori twins both grinned at Jack. He was amazed by how fearless they seemed.

Jack looked back at Captain Day. The captain's face was grim. He shouted something at Jack, but the storm mangled the words. It could have been, "It's your chance!" or "We'll be back!" Jack looked at Cookie. Cookie nodded furiously.

"What?" Jack shouted at Cookie. "What?"

Cookie yelled back, "Don't let go!"

The captain roared something to the twins, something like "Heave him ho!" Toa and Tanati then picked up the wool bale between them, with Jack lying facedown on top of it. They staggered with their load to the gunwale and tottered there a moment. Then they swung Jack on the bale, back and forth.

"Hee—ho—HEE—! HO—!"

They launched Jack and the bale out over the side. Jack screamed. His legs flew up behind him, but he held on. The bale hit the water. Jack went under with it, but he bobbed back up, clinging to the raft of waterproof wool. Jack gripped the rope as the bale pitched and spun. The ship was gone. All was storm now and ocean. The cold ocean water kept slapping Jack's face as his woolly raft spun.

Around, around, and around, the bale raft spun. Jack held on, and he breathed whenever he could. When lightning flashed, he saw bright green sea-foam. Between lightning, he saw nothing but black. The bale bucked and bobbed. Jack kept holding on, trying to keep his face up into the air. He held on and rode the bale until he found himself on top of a mountainous black wave. It lifted Jack so high and so fast that he felt like he was flying. The monster wave lifted him high and higher. Jack took a big breath. The lightning flashed. Thunder roared. Then it all seemed to pause—all of it, the whole ocean and storm. Jack wondered—would he now die?

Then the great wave slowly tipped, and Jack's raft went sliding down the face of it, surfing faster and faster.

When the wave's surface turned to froth, foam and water closed around Jack. He held to the rope as the wave surged between giant black rocks and pitched the raft up onto a hard, dark beach. The remains of the great wave now pulled back toward the ocean. The wool bale started to go with it. Jack weakly let go of the rope and unwound it from his wrist. He rolled off the bale onto the sand. The water sucked at his legs, but it left him where he lay, on his stomach on the hard sand. Jack lay gasping, gulping air, too weak to raise his head. Smaller waves washed his face. Jack choked and coughed, but remained able to breathe.

The next morning brought the island under a quiet blue sky. Moxie and the other young dogs were gathered around old Sage. Sage was ancient. He was immensely wise. His face was so shaggy that it was hard to see he was blind.

The young sheep dogs loved Sage. They chanted, "Tell us a story, Sage, sir. A story, a story!"

"You—want a story?" Sage teased.

"A story! A story!"

"A story about—?"

"About humans!" Moxie yipped quickly. Those were the best stories. And this morning especially, she did not want to hear about fangos.

"Well, now, the humans?" said old Sage. "Well, yes, they

were something. And they were something strange. First strange thing was—it was how they walked. They walked on their hind paws! To us sheep dogs, it seemed their heads were high up in clouds. And truth is, sometimes the father humans made their own clouds. A father human stuck a stick of wood into his mouth. Then he started a little fire inside it. Then he puffed out little clouds of smoke. That smoke smelled wonderful because it meant the father human was happy. And as he chewed on his stick like a dog chews on a bone, the father human growled a happy, humming growl. Oh, everything was fine then, for dogs and the humans. The humans were much like us sheep dogs, and they were our good friends."

"Tell us how they barked!" a pup who liked to bark asked old Sage.

"Oh. They barked whenever they were happy or excited. Sure, they made a lot of other mouth sounds—to us dogs and to each other—but it was only when they were happy or excited that they really let go and had themselves a good long bark."

"Humans were barkers!" a young heeler yipped, although she had heard this before. "And did they howl?"

"Oh. How they howled. They howled when they were happy. They howled when they were sad. And on one special morning every week, they stood in a circle and joined their front paws. And then they all lifted their faces and howled together in a way that was grand."

"And they whistled?"

"Yes, they did," said Sage. "They whistled like birds. It was magical, irresistible to us dogs."

"And their mouths," urged a gray pup with a torn ear. "Tell us about their mouths."

"Well, now," Sage said slowly. "Each human had three mouths. One real mouth was like ours, although not as useful. The other two mouths—they had them on the ends of their front legs! Right where we have our paws. And each of these paw–mouths had five long, soft teeth. These teeth were all covered with skin, and the humans could wiggle and move them. The paw–mouths were useful and they were amazing. The humans were always using them to chew at things. And they used their paw–mouths to scratch us dogs behind our ears in ways that were most enjoyable."

Sage paused. Then he said, "Oh, yes. And the humans loved sticks."

"Sticks!" the young dogs shouted. "Dogs love sticks, too!"

"Yes, sticks," Sage said. "The humans did more with sticks than just smoke them. We dogs trained the humans how to throw sticks. All we had to do was drop sticks at their feet. The humans would throw all the sticks we wanted to chase after. And when they got tired, they would growl and grumble, but they did not seem able to stop themselves. They just had to throw sticks."

Moxie quivered with excitement, trying to imagine a flying stick.

"Oh, yes and yes," old Sage said. "A human was more than just a dog's best friend."

"Tell us more!" the young dogs urged him. "Tell us more!"

The heeler prompted, "What did you call the humans sometimes?" They had all heard this story.

"Well," Sage said. "Sometimes, in fun, we called the humans Stinkers."

The young dogs all howled. "Stinkers! You called them Stinkers!"

"We did," Sage said. "And sure, we loved them. And we loved their magnificent stink. But we also called them our masters, and they deserved that name, too. They were noble creatures, brave and marvelous."

"Stinkers!" barked the pup who liked to bark.

"Of course. They would sweat," said Sage, "like sheep sweat. But their sweat smelled of hard work and high hopes and good humor. The humans were strange, silly, smelly, wonderful creatures. If they weren't working, they were playing. If they weren't playing, they were eating. Or sleeping. Or barking at us dogs. Or barking at each other. They were much like dogs. Like dogs, yes, and different. And still, today, a dog can go to the rock ruins and sometimes—after a rain—catch the scent of the humans."

"Stinkers!" the pup barked. "Stinkers! Stinkers!"

"Yes," Sage said. "After a rain, sometimes—" He grew quiet. He grew lost in remembering.

Big Kelso, the leader dog, had come up during the stories. He had been listening to Sage in a restless, disapproving manner. Moxie saw that Kelso was getting ready to end the fun, so she quickly asked Sage what she always wanted to hear. "What happened to the humans?"

Sage shook his big hairy head. "Moxie, you know they are gone. They left after the fire burned down the house and barn. This was so long ago that I am the only dog left alive who ever knew a human. Now I am blind. That is why I tell you all the time that we must watch for the humans. Because they will come back."

"They'll come back," Moxie said to the other young dogs. "The humans have to come back."

"You must watch for them, Moxie," said old Sage. "They will return."

Kelso now growled low, and the young dogs got quiet.

"Humans," Kelso said. "Humans are gone. They are gone. Gone, and as well as they never were here. But we dogs are here. And so are the fangos."

Moxie cringed at their name.

"The fangos killed another sheep last night," Kelso said. "As hard as we fought them, they still got in and killed one."

"Then we can eat!" yipped the little barker, but Kelso glared at him so fiercely that he fell down and rolled over.

Kelso then glared at all the young dogs. None returned his gaze, but Moxie watched him out of the corner of her eye. Something here was troubling to Kelso.

"The humans are gone, but the fangos remain," Kelso said at last. His tone became fatherly. "So vigilance is the word. Vigilance forever. You must learn to be dogs and watch for the fangos. Always protect the flock."

Kelso turned and trotted away to patrol the edge of the meadow. A few of the young dogs now nervously muttered, "Fangos!" Some of them whispered, "Vigilance!" They held their heads low as they spoke. They warily looked down the meadow, into the dark of the forest.

But the day was bright, and there was something in the air. It made Moxie shake off her fear. She would do something. She would go again to the beach and look for humans. She trotted down through the sloping meadow toward the forest and the ocean. She knew the fangos slept in the day-time, if they slept at all. Moxie imagined that fangos slept with their yellow eyes open.

Moxie started at the spring and followed its small stream down through the grass. The stream entered the forest, where the grass stopped growing and where the sunlight rarely dappled the ground. Deeper in, the forest began to smell like death. It was all bare tree trunks and bare brush and rotting leaves. All of it was woven thickly together, and Moxie had to follow the stream and jump from stone to stone to move through it swiftly. She ducked her head and kept quiet as she moved through the place of the fangos. At the bottom of the forest, the stream fell into a ravine. There, grass again grew, and Moxie felt better. After the stream left the ravine, it crossed a wide, sandy beach and flowed into the ocean.

4

When Jack awoke in the sand, the sun was already high. He sat up. He was stiff and sore, but he felt like he had been sleeping for days. He was on a narrow white beach beneath gray, grass-topped sea-cliffs. The tide was out, but not far.

Between Jack and the ocean, the wet beach mirrored the sky. Beyond the breakers, the sea current swept past in a great torrent. Jack's gaze followed the current as it rushed along the beach. The beach was swept clean, as though by a great broom. The wool bale he had ridden had been washed away, too. No sign remained of the schooner *Patty B*. No planks, no canvas. No bodies, either.

No bodies—that's good, Jack thought. But it was good and it wasn't. He had seen in the storm that many of the sailors were washed overboard. Now, no bodies on the beach meant that the currents were ferocious. *I was lucky,* Jack thought.

He was lucky and he wasn't. He was alone, and he did not know what had become of the *Patty B.* Jack looked around, and he felt just how alone he was.

All around Jack and up and down the beach, great gray rocks rose from the sand and leaned away from the sea-cliffs. To Jack's eye, these rocks looked like crude statues of giant people. They were leaning here and standing there—as though waiting for something—and watching out to the sea. This made Jack look again to the water, to see his ship or some wreckage. He saw nothing but the cheerless blue deep.

Jack stood. He stretched his sore body. He began to walk along the bright beach in the direction of the current, dragging his feet through the sand. He was bone tired, and ached in his shoulders and his chest. He had only what he was wearing—a torn striped shirt, a pair of ragged canvas shorts that hung past his knees, and Tanati's leather belt, which was much too long for him. He had almost nothing, and he was beginning to feel hungry. He felt hungry and alone, and inside he was beginning to feel afraid. But then something made him stop walking. It was more than new fear—it was old sadness. As he realized it, a sudden shudder shook him all over. Jack understood that he had just been orphaned for the second time.

Jack shuddered again, this time on purpose. He wouldn't think about that now. He proceeded on, stumbling along the beach until it disappeared where the sea-cliffs rose straight out of the sea. Jack turned back and began to follow his own footprints. But he noticed how quickly the waves were erasing all the signs of his passing. It was almost as though he too were disappearing. Suddenly his throat tightened, and a great sob burst through it. He thought about Cookie and the captain and about Toa and Tanati. Where were they? There was nothing to be seen of the *Patty B.* There was water and wildness, and that was all.

5

As soon as Moxie got past the fango forest, she shook her coat to rid herself of its fear. The fangos were so doglike, yet so dangerous and wild. The forest was like a night, and the fangos lived in it as nightmares. But below the forest and the fangos lay the ocean at morning and all its possibilities. *They will come from the sea,* Moxie kept thinking. *The humans will come from the sea.*

Moxie came to where the wet sand mirrored the white, splashing surf. Here, enormous rocks leaned away from the sea-cliffs. She thought the great gray forms looked like giant dogs leaning forward on their haunches, watching the wide ocean for the humans to come. Through generations of sheep dogs, the giant rock dogs had waited. Foam and salt water had swirled around their paws.

Moxie trotted along the water's edge. *Nothing,* she thought. *Nothing.* She scanned the wide ocean. She sniffed the ocean breeze. *Nothing. Nothing.* Then she smelled something different. She trotted around one of the great brooding dog rocks and came upon a strange depression in the shiny wet sand. She stopped and stared at it. It looked like a paw print, yet it was the strangest single track she had seen in her life.

It was longer than a dog's paw, and it had five toes instead of four. And it had no sharp claw marks at the ends of the toes. Whatever this creature was, it had no claws. A small wave washed over the print, and it became less distinct. What was this mark in the sand, filling with water? The sight of it transfixed Moxie.

She lowered her nose and sniffed it. Then she sniffed it again. A great excitement began to stir in her heart. Here, among the odors of salt, birds, and rotting kelp, Moxie sensed another, amazing aroma. It was a new smell—a sweet, sweat smell—and thoroughly wondrous.

A small wave washed under Moxie's nose. It almost wiped away what remained of the mysterious print. Worse, the seawater was taking away nearly all of the strange new scent. Moxie could now barely hold on to it, in the back chambers of her nose. She couldn't let it go! She had to salvage it. Quickly, she flopped down on top of the dent in the sand. She rolled over onto her back, and she squirmed back and forth to get all that was left of the scent to stick to her coat.

When Jack came around the rock, he couldn't tell what he was seeing. It looked like a furry kit of black-and-white bagpipes, flopping around in the wet sand. Jack slowly walked toward it. It wasn't until he got within twenty feet of it that he realized it was a little dog. She was vigorously rubbing her back into something in the sand, arching her spine and squirming. The little dog looked funny to Jack. Better than funny—she looked like a lifesaver. *Where there are dogs,* Jack thought, *there are always people.* Where there are people, there is rescue. Jack laughed and clapped his hands.

"Hello, there!" he called.

7

Moxie almost wet herself. She jumped to her feet. What was this? She whirled around to see. What was it? There it was! It—it was—a what?

Moxie fell down. She got up. Her legs wobbled, and she fell. She got ready to run, and she looked back over her shoulder. Now the sight of it stopped her, and she stared at the creature. It was up on its back legs, and it looked all out of balance, but it was somehow managing not to fall. It was tall and gangly and thin and almost hairless. One patch of dark fur grew out of the top of its head. Two smaller strips of fur were stuck on its forehead, just above its large eyes. The rest of this creature's skin seemed to be bald. It had a bald, flat face and a small pug nose *if* one could call that a nose. Its mouth was small. Its teeth were small and square. And its jaw stuck out oddly below its mouth, instead of going straight back to its throat, the way a dog's jaw did.

Not only was this creature hairless, but it wore ragged sheets of some dirty material. The cloth hung from the creature's shoulders and was wrapped around its hips and both of its hind legs. And—this was stranger—the creature's two front legs were hanging loosely down from its shoulders, as though both of its front legs had been broken. At the ends of these free-swinging, broken-looking front legs, the creature had hairless paws, with toes that had been stretched long and had no claws. What was this creature that the sea had thrown up on the beach? Whatever it was, it now began tottering toward Moxie. Moxie slunk low into the wet sand. She was ready to run and wanted to disappear, but the creature kept advancing. Then the creature stopped. Then it barked.

It barked?

Moxie was mystified. Or maybe it didn't bark, but it made a weird, wild sound from the mouth in its hairless, flat face. Then it barked again, and it waved its two crazy front legs in the air. Then its lower legs began to bend, and its body lowered, and the creature bared a mouthful of white, square teeth. It reached out one of its long front legs toward Moxie.

Moxie tried to run, but at first she couldn't get started. She spun in a circle, spraying sand all around. When she found traction, she shot off, and sand sprayed behind her all the way along the beach, back toward the ravine. As she ran, she could hear the creature barking behind her. The creature was barking and baying and howling after her in the most frightening way. But then the creature whistled, high and loud, and the whistle made Moxie stop so fast that she somersaulted through the sand.

She turned and looked back at the creature, and she saw it was still waving its forelegs. It then put its forepaws to its mouth, and it whistled again, and Moxie felt an almost irresistible desire to go back to it. But this feeling scared Moxie even more, and she turned away again and ran even harder, into the ravine, into the forest, and up along the stream.

What was this creature? Moxie ran in frightened wonder. As she dashed through the dark forest, she tried to think how she would describe it to Sage and Kelso. It was tall. It was gangly. It barked and it whistled.

Whistled?

Wait a minute! she thought now. *It whistled?*

It *had* whistled. Moxie slowed her running as the realization broke over her. The creature might be what old Sage was always telling about and what Moxie was always wishing for. The creature might be a human.

But at the same moment that this thought entered Moxie's mind, she trotted straight into a pack of fangos.

The fangos snarled and snapped and gnashed their teeth at her, but Moxie ran hard again and she sped quickly past them. She had surprised them and was gone so quickly that none of the fangos thought to chase her. Moxie raced on. In seconds, she burst into the meadow. She saw the sheep and the dogs up on the hillside near the old rock ruins. She tore through the green grass and leaped from rock to rock. She sped toward them full tilt until her wind gave out, and she slowed to a ragged trot. She reached the sheep, passed the other dogs, and searched the meadow until she found old Sage near a section of broken rock wall. Sage had his nose to the breeze. Moxie tried to speak, but she couldn't. She was too winded and too excited. She panted in rasps of burning breath.

But Sage understood. "A human?" he said.

Jack followed the Border collie's tracks up the beach to where she had dashed into a ravine. He thought he could track her to her home, and there he would find people.

People! Jack thought. That made him feel happier, but suddenly he felt sadder, too. He felt he needed to fall apart and to cry over the captain and Cookie and the brave Maori twins, but at the moment his hope for rescue was near to overpowering. And maybe—Jack hoped—he would find something even better! The people would tell him there were other survivors of the *Patty B.* Or better yet—he grinned now—he would find the good captain and the twins and Cookie, all waiting for him, sipping tea in a farm wife's cozy house.

Jack brightened as the sunlight dimmed and he moved deeper into the forest. Soon he lost the little dog's trail, but he came upon a small stream. The brush and trees on either side of it grew thick and too tangled to walk through, so Jack followed the stream higher by jumping from stone to stone.

Jack came to a place where the ground leveled off. The brush grew even thicker here, and the tree canopy grew bigger. An ugly, rotten smell sifted through the foliage. *Something bad here,* Jack thought. He wondered whether he should leave the stream and strike straight up through the forest. It was then, as he was resting, breathing hard and looking around, that he suddenly felt surrounded.

There were animals near. He could not see them, but he smelled them. They had a bad smell, a strange smell, like rotten meat. And now he heard them moving and snuffling in the leaves and shadows. At first, Jack thought they might be wild boars. Then three of the animals stepped out into the clearing.

They were dogs. Or, no—not normal dogs. Jack stepped back, and they all stepped forward, into a shaft of pale light. They were like a sort of dog, but a wild kind. They made Jack think of dingos and jackals. They were all different from each other in some way, like in their size and coat color and the length of their hair. But they were all alike in that they were scarred and soiled, with mangy and matted coats, and their eyes were dull yellow. Their eyes showed no sign that they saw Jack as a human. Their eyes showed no feelings at all. A chill fell down Jack's spine and he looked back over his shoulder. Five more wild dogs had ranged in behind him. Others had appeared on both sides. Some of these creatures were smaller, and some larger, than the first three Jack had seen. They, too, were of different builds, but all of them shared that wild yellow look. Some were panting, their tongues lolling out of their mouths and dripping, but none of them made a sound. One of the closer ones yawned, and the way he yawned threatened Jack more with its absolute disdain.

Then the wild dog who had yawned suddenly whined and the others shifted and cowered. They slunk their heads low, as another creature appeared in the clearing.

This creature was larger than the others and more power-ful looking, and yet more gaunt and gruesome. Some sec-onds passed before Jack realized he was a wild dog, too. He looked like he might be a shepherd or wolf hound, but it seemed to Jack that life had treated him even worse than it had his companions. His face had many scars and white whiskers; his ribs showed through his ragged, scurfy coat; and his shoulder blades stuck out sharply. He looked ancient. He snarled at the others as he stepped into the middle of the clearing. He sat back on his haunches and looked around at all of them, as though to count them or to warn them to know their places. He had those same dead-yellow, stone-cold eyes.

Then he looked at Jack, and his expression changed. His head jerked more upright. He stood back up on all four feet, and he studied Jack closely. Into the wild dog's eyes came a spark of recognition.

This spooked Jack. "Hey!" he said. "Hey! Go!" Jack waved his arms. But the wild creature kept studying him.

"Scat!" Jack shouted. But the creature took a step closer.

"Go!" Jack felt the danger. These were the most frightening creatures Jack had ever seen. Quickly, he looked around for a club, but the ground held nothing but brown leaves and dead twigs.

Then the creature stepped closer again, and so did the others. What could Jack do? If he ran, they would be on him in a flash. If he fought, he would not last long. He looked around again. His only hope was up in the trees. Just above him he saw a limb reaching down from a sturdy trunk. Jack grabbed the limb and pulled himself up on top of it. He shinned his way along it to the trunk of the tree. There he sat on the limb and leaned his back against the tree. He felt a thrill of escape, but it vanished quickly. The limb was so narrow that it was hard to keep balanced. Below him, the wild dogs had already moved in closer. Some sat on their haunches and watched him, dully but directly. Others appeared to pay Jack no attention at all. But it was obvious that they were waiting for him to climb down or to fall. The pack's leader watched Jack with close, unnerving interest.

Kelso and three other sheep dogs had come up to Moxie and old Sage.

"Well?" Kelso asked. Moxie still could not catch her breath. Her tongue hung from her mouth, wagging and dripping.

"What is it?" Kelso asked. More dogs were gathering around.

"It—!" was all that Moxie could pant.

"It what?" Kelso said.

"It—is here!" Moxie gasped.

"What is here?" Kelso asked old Sage. There was a moment of no sound except for Moxie's panting.

Then Sage cleared his throat.

"It is a human," Sage said.

"A human!" All of the dogs said this at once. "A human!"

"Come near. Smell the human on her," Sage said. The dogs came forward, and they all sniffed the new scent that suffused Moxie's coat. Electricity ran through the pack.

"A human! Where is it?" they all began to ask her. "Where!? What does it look like? How tall? How brave? How strong? Show us! Show us!"

All Moxie could do was look down toward the forest.

10

Jack struggled to keep his balance on top of the tree limb, and he knew he couldn't keep it for long. He was tired already, and his fatigue made him tremble until he almost lost his grip. He needed rest, but if he relaxed or fell asleep, he would certainly fall off the limb. Below Jack, the wild dogs waited patiently, some watching, some yawning, some even sleeping with an open eye. Their dull, hungry, indirect attention looked as though it would last forever.

For the second time in two days, Jack wondered if he would die. This time he wondered: What would that feel like? Would it hurt? Surely it would. But Jack could not imagine that now. What he felt more clearly was the hard discomfort of the rough bark beneath him. Jack adjusted his position and almost fell. New fear shot through his ragged nerves. But at least he felt alive. Jack looked down at the pack leader, who was now staring almost straight up at Jack. With his skeletal body and his stony yellow eyes, the wild dog looked like he was both alive and dead.

"Well," Jack called down to the dog, and he suddenly thought of a name. "Well, Mr. Bones," he said. "You think you've got me."

Mr. Bones' eyes did not change, but he cocked his head at the sound of Jack's voice. It was almost as though he recognized Jack and knew him.

This angered Jack. "Well, you haven't got me, Mr. Bones," he said. "You haven't. I'll die up here first."

And that gave Jack an idea. He still had his belt. It had been a gift from Tanati. It was long and very strong. He could belt himself to the limb. Then, after many hours, or even after some days, the wild dogs might grow tired and leave him, and he could climb down. And if these dogs never went away—well then, they would never get him, ever, if he remained belted to the tree.

With his right hand, Jack let go of the limb and reached down to his belt buckle to carefully unfasten it. He slowly pulled the long belt out of its belt loops. At the end, he had to shake it to get it to come free. Then Jack flipped the buckled end up over his back and around the limb below him. He let go of the branch with his other hand and, balancing on his stomach, he reached down and felt around for the belt's end. He grabbed it and slipped it through the buckle. He pulled it as tight as he could and then pushed the buckle's prong into the hole in the leather. It was secure. It felt good.

"Well, well, Mr. Bones," Jack said more confidently than before. He pulled on the belt end to tighten it further. But just as he pushed the prong into a new hole, Jack shifted, and he lost his balance.

"Ahhh—!" Jack rolled off the limb. He fell, but the belt caught him, and it rolled him around and under the limb. He hung under the tree limb with his back facing down, his spine arching backward and his head, hands, and heels bouncing in the air.

"Ahhh—!" Pain seared his spine, and he saw black sparks. Jack cried out again and writhed in his pain. He flailed beneath the limb until he got himself turned around. The pain eased, but now Jack was hanging facedown.

All the wild dogs were gathering beneath him. Mr. Bones jumped up and bit at him. Jack pulled back his arms. Mr. Bones missed. His jaws popped together like two blocks of wood, his body twisted in the air as he fell back to the ground, and he landed on his side with an ugly thud. Slowly, with his ribs swelling, Mr. Bones rose to his feet and then, just as slowly, he sat back on his haunches. Mr. Bones waited below Jack, with all his bad partners around him.

Jack hung from his belt, holding his feet and hands up out of reach, but he knew he could not keep them that way for long. This is it, he thought. This is the end. And the end, he knew, would be bad.

But then, below him, the wild dogs suddenly jerked their heads. They all turned in the same direction and looked up the little stream. Several held up their noses and sniffed. One whined, then another. Something had changed. Then one of them—then all except Mr. Bones—glided away into the darkness of the forest.

Mr. Bones now stood still, staring up at Jack. Then he looked back up the stream, and he too disappeared. Jack quickly took his chance to pull at the belt buckle. It released, and he hit the ground hard. When he could raise his head, Jack looked around, and he saw he was surrounded by another pack of dogs. But this pack was completely different. These were fine animals—shepherds, collies, heelers, and sheep dogs.

Jack sat up. Then he stood, holding his belt with one hand and the waist of his shorts with the other. He looked around at the dogs. Their eyes were bright. Their coats were glossy. Their noses were wet and shiny. Among them he saw the little black-and-white Border collie that he had met on the beach. He noticed now that her eyes were of two colors—one blue, one brown. They gave her face an intelligent appearance, as though she could see things in more than one way.

Jack raised his hand to her in greeting. But without a belt to hold them up, his shorts fell down around his knees. Jack laughed at himself. He reached down for his shorts.

"Just a moment, here, gang," he said to the dogs. But when he straightened back up, all the sheep dogs were gone, except for one big, noble-looking German shepherd. He watched Jack for another full minute. Then he turned and trotted away.

II

Nearly all the other dogs beat Moxie back to the meadow. When she arrived, everyone there was in a state of great excitement. They bounded in circles around Sage. Some of the younger pups were so worked up that they were chasing their own tails.

"So—" Sage said to the older dogs. "Tell me."

"Oh! It's a human!" one dog said.

"It's a human!" said another.

"No, it's not," another said. "It's scrawny, weak, and ugly."

"It's pitiful," another said. "It can't be a human."

"Then what is it?" Sage asked.

"Maybe it's a half-human?" one said. "You know. It's like what a fango is to a dog."

"Yes!" said another dog. "It's like what a nightmare is to a dream."

"No, no," said another. "I think it is a human. It's a human, but it has something wrong with it."

While the sheep dogs were all talking, Kelso came trotting up through the meadow. When he arrived, the dogs all became quiet.

Old Sage sensed Kelso's presence. "Well, Kelso," Sage said. "What do you think this new creature is?"

Kelso took his place beside Sage. "I don't know what it is," he said to Sage. Then he said to all of the dogs, "But I know what a dog is. A dog is brave. A dog is vigilant. A dog will protect the sheep." Kelso paused, then he went on. "And we will protect the sheep. Always. Even from this new creature."

The sheep dogs now turned to old Sage.

"The creature is a human," Sage said. "A human pup called a boy."

Sage raised his nose again. He had caught a scent on the breeze. "And we now should welcome the boy."

Moxie and the other dogs then turned and looked down the meadow to see that the boy had emerged from the trees. They watched him run out into the meadow and stop when he saw the dogs. The boy raised one of his front legs and waved it over his head. Many of the dogs gasped when they saw him do this. Then the boy took a step, and he fell. Then he got up, and he fell again. He got up once more, and he came running up toward them, through the meadow. The boy was awkward. His front legs milled in the air. Some of the sheep dogs backed up, thinking that the boy might be attacking.

"Are you sure that's a human?" Kelso asked Sage. "Can humans be so clumsy?"

Old Sage could not see, but he knew humans. "Boy humans, especially, can be clumsy," he said.

The boy now apparently stubbed his toe on a rock. He stopped and hopped up and down, holding his foot. Then, more carefully, he resumed his running. The sheep dogs watched him with a mixture of horror and fascination.

"Let's go meet him!" some said.

"Is he dangerous?" said others.

12

After tripping again, Jack got back to his feet. He was thrilled by what he saw. He was in a great green meadow sloping up to a rocky hill crest. A flock of sheep grazed near the top of the meadow. And just below the sheep, a pack of sheep dogs was standing in a loose bunch, all looking down at him. Behind the dogs, the remains of an old rock wall rose out of the grass, and it ran back out of sight over a hill. The sheep, the dogs, and the wall could mean only one thing. People! Jack waved at the dogs and began running again. As he ran, he called out, "Hello! Hello! Hey! Hey!"

Half of the dogs now came bounding down the meadow toward him. Behind them followed several puppies, who tripped and tumbled through the grass. When the dogs reached him, they surrounded him and ran around him in circles. At the edge of the circle, Jack saw the little black-and-white Border collie.

"Hello, dogs!" Jack said to all of them. "Hello again!" he said to the little collie. "I'm happy to see you. Where are your masters? Up there?" He pointed over the hill, to beyond the rock wall. With the dogs running all around him, Jack hiked up through the meadow. Near the top, in front of the flock of sheep, there stood the big German shepherd Jack had seen in the woods and an old gray-and-white English sheep dog with hair over his eyes.

"You must be the boss," Jack said to the German shepherd.

"You must be the grandfather," Jack said to the sheep dog.

"And the people—?" Jack continued. "They must be over this hill."

Jack passed between the two dogs, and he climbed to where the old stone wall began as a loose pile of stones. With rising excitement, he followed the wall. Over the top, he expected to find a house. He expected smoke rising from a chimney, and guinea fowl in a yard, and children and a mother wiping her hands on her apron, and a father, maybe working on a plow or smoking his pipe and smiling up at Jack.

But when Jack got to the top, he stopped. He stood looking down into a gentle green swale that lay between him and the final rise before the top of the sea-cliffs. There in front of him, he saw a sight that at first thrilled him and then shivered him through. He saw ruins—the ruined remains of a farmstead. There was nothing but the broken rock walls of what had been a house and a barn, now in the last stage of collapse to the ground. Brush and briars climbed what remained of the walls. Burned and blackened beams lay crisscrossed in jumbles, with the brush growing up through them and sprouting little red flowers. There was nothing else—no sign that any people had been there in a very long time. Even the path that must have run between the house and barn had been long grown over with grass.

Jack turned to look behind him. Many of the dogs had followed.

"Where are the people?" he demanded. He waved his arms toward the ruins. But the dogs looked at Jack as though he were getting stranger.

"Well, OK," Jack said. "I'm sure they'll be coming before dark. From somewhere, right? They have to bring the sheep in. Right?"

The dogs all watched him. Some held their heads cocked to one side.

"Then right!" Jack said to them. And to himself, he said, "Right-o!"

The happiness of a near rescue returned to Jack, but

with a sense of fragility. He looked all around. It was, at the least, very beautiful here. The sun shone bright. The breeze blew warm. The meadows glowed, green and blooming with colors.

Jack saw the little Border collie waiting at the edge of the other dogs. "Here, girl!" he called, but she would not come.

Jack walked through the ruins and from there up to the hill crest. The wind lifted his hair as he walked over the top. In front of him, the great cliff fell away to the sea, and the sea stretched away to the horizon. Jack climbed on a large, flat rock for a better view. From there, he saw something that made him uneasy again.

Across the water, he could just barely make out through the low ocean haze the coast of a bigger land beneath a long white cloud. Jack jumped off the rock and clambered up a taller one. He stood as tall as he could. He turned and he turned again, scanning the horizon. The haze was not heavy. Jack saw it all plainly now. He was on an island. Could he be all alone?

Jack looked back down at the dogs and their sheep. He now noticed the sheep's fleeces were dirty and matted. It looked like they had never been sheared.

Jack's spirits fell lower with the night. He shivered from the cold, inside and out. He lay down and curled up behind some bushes at the base of the rock wall. He did not know if the dogs were watching over him. He hoped they were, but he kept his eyes shut as hard as he could. He covered his ears to keep from hearing a high, drifting, whiny howling, which he thought probably came from the wild dogs in the forest. As the night slowly passed, Jack tried to sleep, but every time he drifted off, he had to wake again to change position.

Finally sleep came. In his dream, Jack heard the captain order the Maori twins to heave Jack into the sea.

"Heave him!" the captain roared. "Heave him ho!" The memory unreefed in a dream and unfurled like a sail.

"Hee—! Ho—!" Toa and Tanati swung Jack over the side. Jack again felt the flying, falling feeling of being thrown from the ship; of being tossed on the black waves; and of hitting the hard, hard sand. He awoke on the cold ground by the falling-down rock wall, and he ached in his very soul.

13

By his second day on the island, Jack was sure he was alone. There was nothing newly built here, no fresh signs of people. Every human-made thing was burnt out and grown over. For some reason, the sheep dogs were still here, and they were still guarding the sheep. In their way, these sheep dogs were the island's sole civilization. But where had the people gone? When were they coming back? Why did the dogs herd the sheep and move them around for pasture? The sheep dogs were no doubt protecting the sheep against the savage dogs in the forest. But why?

Also, the sheep dogs did not treat Jack the way he would expect to be treated by dogs. The pups and younger dogs continued to follow him around, but only the youngest pups allowed him to touch them. Even then, the mothers came to nudge the puppies away. The younger dogs ran up to Jack, but they shied whenever he reached down to pet them. Some dogs—the heelers, mainly—had taken to playing a kind of tag with Jack, in which they ran up behind him and nipped at his heels and his bottom. Others—the Border collies— tried to hypnotize him, the same way they entranced the sheep with their eyes. They lowered their heads and fixed Jack with their eyes, and after a while, it seemed like it worked. At first Jack thought it was all a game, but then he began to feel that the sheep dogs were trying to control him.

It was strange. On the evening of the first day, several dogs had herded Jack out past the ruins to where there lay the remains of a recently dead sheep. Its carcass had been ripped apart and partly eaten, either by these same sheep dogs or by the evil creatures that had attacked Jack in the forest. Jack wondered at the time what the dogs thought they were doing. Were they leading him to food or showing him what could become of him?

Regardless, Jack was hungry. He would have roasted and eaten some of the sheep, but he had no fire to cook the meat. How would he live now? What would he do? He had to eat. If he waited much longer, the mutton would rot. But the thought of eating raw meat made him gag.

He remembered the cold night he had just spent by the wall. He wished that he could take the fleece off the dead sheep and make himself a cloak. But now, in the sun, Jack was warm again, and the thought of the cloak began to fade. Jack shook his head to keep with the thought, but it vanished with the morning.

Jack wandered along the headland at the top of the seacliffs. Far below him, the swift current rushed past the leaning rocks. The little Border collie still followed him, but she kept her distance. Every time he called or whistled, her ears perked and her head tipped, but she would come no closer. She seemed the nicest and sharpest of all the dogs. Perhaps she was frightened of him, but he could see no good reason. Now, as Jack watched, the little collie turned and trotted away from him. Jack stood so he could keep her in sight as long as possible. He watched her disappear, and then he looked around again at the island. It was alone in the sea. Below him, the current rushed past like a river.

Jack's memories flowed. He thought of Cookie. He smiled, conjuring up the cook's two round eyes and one furry eyebrow. Then Jack saw the wild, tattooed faces of Tanati and Toa and the kindly, resolute face of the captain. *Those were friends,* Jack thought, and now he realized they had been family, too.

"Ah—!" Jack exclaimed. He fell back into the grass. He again felt the swell and toss of the ocean waves. All of it! All of this! It had happened to him. What had happened to his crew? Logic told Jack that they must have drowned. But hope told him that they couldn't have. Hope and the memories of how strong and brave and smart they were. If anyone could have sailed through that storm, then the captain and Cookie and the Maori twins could have.

Jack searched the clouds and found their faces. He blinked rapidly to turn his imagination into a moving scene. It was like a magic lantern show in the orphanage parlor. Jack smiled. This was nice. It was sad, but nice. His crew. The sun. He fell asleep.

14

Moxie left the boy on the ridge top. Was he really a human? If he was, he wasn't doing too many very grand things. He didn't eat. He didn't smoke sticks. He didn't bark much, and when he did bark, it came out quite yippy. Mostly, the boy just walked back and forth and looked out over the ocean. Moxie decided to go down to the ruins to talk with old Sage.

15

Jack dreamed he was back in San Francisco, at St. Brendan's Home for Sea-Stranded Boys. It was Christmas Eve, one year before. A hammering came at the orphanage door, and Jack raced the other boys to get to it first. The boys all waited breathlessly for Father Maley to answer the door, but they weren't expecting Santa Claus. They were all wishing for something better. Sometimes before Christmas, people came to adopt boys.

"ALL RIGHT!" Father Maley was already shouting over his own deafness. "ALL RIGHT, NOW! WHAT?" The boys crowded around him. He threw open the door.

But there was no one there. It had been raining, and it was going to rain again. There was that in-between mist around the gas lamps.

But—no one there. Jack peered out with the other boys.

And then someone! The boys all jumped back. Out of the mist stepped a cheery old wool-coated sailor, chewing on a whalebone pipe. The pipe danced in his grin. A thick rope of blue pipe smoke halfway haloed his head.

"Arrgh!" the man said. Jack grew excited. He thought, *Just like a sailor!*

Jack looked up happily at Father Maley.

"WELL!" the old priest shouted at the sailor.

"WELL?" he shouted again.

Jack saw that the sailor wasn't yet ready to speak. The old salt grinned and puffed and chewed on his pipe. Jack figured he had come up from the Embarcadero, where the ships all tied up with their stories and their cargoes.

"WELL!" Father Maley yelled again.

The old sailor didn't say a word. But he made sure to look each orphan in the eye. They all stared back at him, each trying to look like a "Possible." That was what Father Maley called an orphan good enough for someone to take home. The sailor looked twice at Jack. Each time, Jack tried to return his regard, open-faced and wide-eyed, like the honest boy he was. But each time, Jack couldn't help moving his own face to mimic the old sailor's expressions. The sailor noticed this and smiled.

"WELL!" Father Maley yelled.

The sailor was now grinning. But then he scowled and he mumbled. He chewed on his pipe and seemed to be mulling over something very important. He looked at Jack again and studied him, head to shoes.

Jack met the old sailor's gaze as well as he could. The sailor was short, with a comic square face, which was both merry and stormy. He had a single long, white bushy eyebrow, and Jack saw only three teeth. As the sailor surveyed the boys, his pipe jumped about and jittered. His pipe smoke wound around everyone. Oh, what a picture! The old man looked so happy and so fierce that Jack liked him immediately.

"Mmm—yes!" the sailor said now, his pipe still a-jitter. Then he nodded. His eyebrow arched. He said, "Oh, yes. Oh, yes. Oh, yes."

"Oh, yes!" Jack whispered. He loved that word. Yes.

"WELL?" Father Maley shouted.

Then the old sailor nodded like he had made a decision. His eyebrow bunched up in the middle of his forehead. "Mmm—yes!" the old sailor said. He pointed the stem of his pipe at Jack. The other orphans glanced at Jack with envy.

Then the old sailor pointed his pipe at Father Maley and

jerked it toward the street. He turned away, and Father Maley followed him out into the mist under the streetlamp. Father Maley turned to the boys and gave them a nod.

The boys watched as the two men held their conversation. Father Maley kept shouting "WELL?" The old sailor's smoke hung around them like a Christmas bow.

Jack's heart swelled. He knew that he had been chosen. He shrugged to the other boys in the most respectful way he knew. That's luck, he wanted them to know. Your luck will come. The other boys went back into the parlor, and Jack stood and waited.

That night, Jack was the new cabin boy on board the *Patty B,* helping Cookie make a delicious Christmas Eve supper. For his gifts, the crew provisioned Jack with their old clothes, and the fiercely tattooed but wildly friendly Tanati gave Jack a very long—but plenty good—belt. After supper, the sailors sang carols and drank rum. Then they took turns teasing young Jack. They hid his duffel bag. They tied him all up in his hammock. The teasing made Jack feel so happy that he had to work to pretend that it bothered him.

Jack had a family again. On Christmas day, they sailed.

16

Oh, I'm quite sure the boy is a human," Sage told Moxie.

"But he doesn't *do* anything," Moxie said. "He doesn't even eat."

"Sure, humans eat," Sage said. "We must make certain that he eats."

"But how?" Moxie asked.

Sage thought for a long time and then said, "He is a boy, and so you have to think like a boy in order to engage him. Go now and bring him to me."

"But how?" Moxie asked. "He hates being herded."

"With a stick, of course," answered Sage.

17

Jack had barely woken when he saw the little Border collie trotting back toward him. She carried a stick in her mouth. When she got up close to him, she dropped the stick.

"Hello again," Jack said.

The little dog backed away. She did this in the way Jack had seen many of the Border collies do. They kept their heads low to the ground and their eyes on the sheep. The little Border collie kept looking back and forth between Jack and the stick. She seemed to be willing him to go to the stick.

"You want to play fetch?" Jack said.

The little dog kept watching him.

"Well, all right then, girl." Jack walked forward and picked up the stick. He shouted, "Fetch!" and he flung the stick far out over the little dog's head and into the meadow.

The little dog tore after the stick and came running back with it. But this time she dropped the stick some ten feet away from Jack.

"Bring it closer," Jack said.

But the little dog just backed away from it again.

Jack laughed. "You dumb dog," he said, but he could see she was smart. He snapped his fingers and pointed at the stick. "Fetch!" he commanded. But the little dog stayed. Jack shook his head. "I can see that you're going to take some training." He walked over to the stick, picked it up and threw it again. "Bring it back this time!" he called. The little dog raced away after it.

And again the little dog dropped the stick ten feet from Jack. She backed away and waited for him.

"That won't do," Jack said. This time he stood his ground. He waited. The little dog waited and watched him. And time passed.

"Fetch the stick," Jack said after more minutes had gone by.

This time, the little dog trotted forward. She picked up the stick in her teeth. But she did not bring it to Jack. Instead, she carried it another ten feet farther away. She dropped it again. She backed away and watched him.

"I said, that won't do," Jack said. He started to go after the stick, but then he realized what was happening.

"You're taking me somewhere, aren't you, girl? Where are we going?" he asked. He picked up the stick and threw it again, this time in the direction that the little dog appeared to be leading him.

Again she dropped the stick away from him. After five more throws, they arrived back at the burnt ruins.

"What is it, girl?" Jack asked.

The old English sheepdog was there, sitting alone by the rock wall. The little dog dropped the stick right in front of the old one. Then she backed away.

"Hello, Grandfather," Jack said. He walked up to the old dog, and he knelt and petted his gray head. Then he pushed back the hair on the dog's face to look into his eyes. Jack saw that they were smoky and blind.

"You've seen a lot," Jack said. He rubbed the old dog behind his ears and looked around at the burnt ruins. "I'll bet you know all about what happened here."

The old dog pulled away from Jack and let out a "Woof!" Then the dog moved away a few paces. He turned back to Jack and barked again.

Jack stood. "You leading me, too, Grandfather? Well, lead on, then. I'm coming."

The old blind dog padded through the yard between the ruins of the house and the barn. He waited until Jack came up to him. Jack scratched him again behind the ear. Then the old dog went over to the rock wall, and he put his nose into a rectangular hole in the wall where a stone had fallen out. He pulled his nose back out.

"Woof!" he announced.

"Something in there?" Jack said. He knelt down beside the old dog. He reached into the gap and felt around with his fingers. It was mossy in the hole and damp, but Jack felt something hard in there with square corners, and he pulled it out. It was a rusted metal box with a lid. No lettering left on it—no paint, just rust.

"What's this?" Jack showed the box to the little Border collie, who had trotted up beside him. Her ears were already up. "What is it? Letters? Tools? Money?"

Jack laughed. "Money!" he joked to the old dog. "We can buy us our passage off this island."

Jack sat down on the ground and put the box in his lap. With his fingernails and a sharp stone, he was able to pry off the top. Inside the box, he found treasures: a small folding knife, a man's wooden pipe, a foil pouch with tobacco, and a glass jar full of wooden matches.

"Hooray!" Jack shouted. He held his treasures in the air. "Hooray!" He showed them to the young Border collie. Jack opened the foil tobacco pouch and stuck his nose into it. The tobacco was dried, but the sweet smell of it brought him fond memories of the sailors on his ship.

"This is good," he whispered. "This is very good."

He held the open pouch under the nose of the old sheep dog, and he thought he could see the old dog quiver.

"God bless you, Grandfather," Jack said, and he smelled the tobacco again. "God bless dogs. And God bless people and God bless me!"

Jack didn't try a match right away, but he knew what the matches meant. He could have fire now. He could roast the mutton. He could stay warm at night. He could light a signal fire on the cliff-top. If he could keep the fire going—or keep the coals alive—these matches would last him for as long as he needed them.

Jack leaned back against the stone wall. The hard stones felt warm in the sun. Jack kept his nose in the pouch of the rich tobacco, and he looked around at the island. He thought about what little it takes to be happy sometimes. What a good lot you have when you get one good break. Jack considered it all, and he realized that there was likely much more on this island than he had first thought. If he dug around the burnt ruins, there was no telling what he'd find. Pots and pans. Tools. Even nails to use to build a shelter. And the people who had lived here had no doubt kept a garden. He might find some root crops that still grew there wild. Somewhere nearby, there might even be an orchard. Apples! Pears! Jack's mouth watered with the possibilities.

Although his stomach still ached, it now ached with expectation. He stuck one of the matches into his mouth and enjoyed the taste of the wood. He surveyed the old tumbled walls. What beauty there is in a wall, rising up out of stones. To Jack at this moment, the old wall looked as though it were building itself up, rather than falling down.

Jack saw that where the wall formed a corner, it was stronger, and the top of the wall rose higher. Idly, Jack peered into the corner, admiring its strength, and then something in there caught his eye.

He got up and walked over to see it better.

"Here, now!" he said. "Something else."

It was a walking staff. It was strong and hand-rubbed and about six feet tall. It was leaning there, right where the two walls joined—leaning where someone had left it long ago. Or, no, Jack imagined, the person had not left the staff. The person had put it there, and then for some reason, he had been unable to return to get it.

Or, no, Jack thought now, in his mood of new happiness. *No,* he thought, *the person left the walking staff there for me. He might not have known it at the time, but he did.*

Jack stepped through the low brush and over a few stones to get to the walking staff. He reached into the corner and picked it up. Then he heard a low growl behind him.

The memory of Mr. Bones shot through him in a chill.

Jack spun around with the stick held high, ready to use it as a club. But he saw that the growling was coming from the old blind dog. The old dog wasn't facing Jack, but he kept on growling.

Jack lowered the stick. "What is it, Grandfather?" he asked. "What's the matter?"

The old dog couldn't see him—Jack was sure of that—but all the same, the old dog meant to say something.

"What is it?" Jack said again.

The old dog lowered his head and growled lower and louder. Behind him, the little Border collie came nearer, and she started growling, too. She was obviously growling straight at Jack.

"What, girl? What did I do?" Jack said. Then he looked down at the walking staff in his hands. "Oh," he said. "Oh, right. This was someone else's. It was your master's, Grandfather? You don't want me to have it? But you want me to know about it. Is that it?"

Jack felt that the dogs were about to speak to him. But of course they did not.

"So—right—" Jack said finally. He turned and leaned the walking staff back in its place in the corner.

"Right-o," he said to the two dogs. "There it stays. Thank you for showing me."

It amazed Moxie how quickly the boy changed once Sage had shown him the human things at the wall. First it was the sticks. He started throwing sticks for the dogs. They ran after them, and they played keep-away from each other, and all the while the boy was gathering more sticks and piling them by a great flat rock. The big pile of sticks seemed to be an obsession for him.

Then the boy went to the rock wall and took out one of the human things that Sage had shown him. It was a shiny, pointed thing like a long canine tooth. The boy held the tooth-thing in front of his face and swished it back and forth through the air. Moxie got ready to run because she thought he might throw it like a stick.

But the boy carried the tooth-thing over to the carcass of the sheep that the fangos had killed. He knelt down by the carcass and spent some time staring at it, looking like he didn't know quite what to do. Then, holding the tooth-thing at the end of one of his forelegs, the boy began to use it to work at the carcass.

What was this? The meat cut apart! The tooth-thing was indeed a tooth. The boy used it to tear and slice and pull apart the sheep meat in a way that would take two dogs with strong jaws to match. It seemed strange to Moxie that the boy never used the mouth in his face except to growl quietly to himself.

Then the boy carried a whole side of the sheep's ribs back to the big stick pile and built a smaller pile of sticks nearby.

By now, the sun was going down, and the sky was getting dark. The boy used another human something to start a light flickering in the sticks. This light blazed up, and the dogs all gathered to watch. They thrilled to the light, and they drew in to the warmth of the blaze. It felt oddly natural to Moxie. The boy appeared overjoyed. The dogs watched the boy as he danced and howled and carried on around the roaring fire.

Moxie sat, watching, between Sage and Kelso.

Sage said, "Tell me, Kelso. Is the creature acting a little crazy?"

"Far beyond that," Kelso said. "I think he has gone mad."

"That takes away my last doubt, then," Old Sage said. "He is indeed a boy."

"He is amazing!" Moxie exclaimed. Her eyes were wide. She knew she could not yet bring herself to go right up to the boy, but she knew she wanted to, more than anything.

"The boy is a problem," Kelso said, and he looked back down the meadow toward the black forest, where the fangos were surely skulking. "The boy is clumsy and stupid and helpless, and he is probably unlucky for us."

"Not so," old Sage said. "Boys are lucky. Human pups are the luckiest animals alive."

The three sheep dogs watched the boy dancing by the fire.

"Lucky for himself, perhaps, but he is unlucky for us," Kelso said. "We sheep dogs have now lived without humans for long enough that we have learned to live like true dogs do. We are noble. We are free. We are vigilant and brave. We have become ourselves by keeping to ourselves. We have it good now—all except for the war with the fangos—and even that war keeps us true.

"And now," Kelso continued, "I see the young dogs changing around the boy. Now they like him. Soon they will love him. And then what? What's next? Will they worship him? And obey him? Whatever he wants them to do, they will do. And they will forget what it means to be a dog—and free."

Old Sage let out a long, slow breath. "Maybe a human gives meaning to a dog. Maybe a dog needs a human to be true."

"Vigilance is our truth," Kelso said, and he stood and turned to scan the forest line for fangos.

But Moxie could not keep her eyes off the boy, who continued to dance and howl around the fire. He was loud. He was wild. And yet he could stop his wildness when he needed to and work at the fire. Moxie felt drawn to join in the boy's wildness and compelled to help him in his work, if only she could.

The boy held his front legs up above his head and whirled in circles. He had propped the rack of sheep meat with some rocks near the flames. As Moxie now watched, the boy stopped his dancing to reposition the meat. Then he ripped a small strip of meat free from the ribs, and he threw that piece to one of the dogs. The dog caught it in the air and shook it with glee. That made the boy make his funny, happy barking sounds. The boy slapped his forepaws on his knees and stamped his hind feet. Then the boy turned, and he noticed Moxie. He pointed one of his forepaws at her. Then he put the other forepaw to his mouth and he whistled.

It made Moxie jump up and start running toward the boy.

"Wait!" Kelso yipped, but Moxie was running. She was halfway to the boy before she realized what she was doing. She tried to stop—front feet first—and she tumbled through a somersault.

The boy made more happy barking when he saw this, and he slapped his forepaws together. Then he whistled again, and the piping power of that sound popped Moxie up again, and she was running to the boy. She ran right up to him, and she would have leaped right into his forelegs, but he suddenly showed his teeth.

She stopped. What was this? What did he mean by the teeth? Then the boy showed more teeth, and he barked the happy barks. Then he ripped off a strip of the cooking mutton, and he tossed it at Moxie. Moxie tried to get out of its way, but it hit her on her nose and slavered warm meat juice all over it. Moxie licked her nose, and she found that the warm meat juice was the most delicious taste she had ever experienced. She sniffed at the meat on the ground. The smell of it made her mouth open. Out came her tongue, and she licked the meat, and before she knew it the whole piece of meat jumped right into her mouth.

Oh! Delicious! Now Moxie was trying to swallow it whole, before any of the other dogs could get a bite of it.

Turning and turning away from the other dogs' mouths, Moxie finally got the meat swallowed down. So good! She looked back at the boy. He was pointing one of his forelegs at her. He had his head back and his mouth open, and those short happy barks were coming out of his mouth. Moxie cocked her head and watched him and listened. His odd barking sounds were truly joyful. Then the boy howled and clapped his forepaws together, and several of the younger dogs began howling, too. And now Moxie joined in—she could not help herself.

Ow-wooooo! Ow-wooooo!

What a delight. What a joy in life. All along the old rock wall, the firelight made great shadows jump as the boy and the young dogs danced late into the night.

In the morning, while the boy was gathering more sticks, the younger dogs began pestering old Sage. They wanted to know more about humans and dogs.

And about fangos.

"A fango story! The fangos!" the young heeler yipped.

Moxie cringed. She did not want to hear about fangos.

"Well, then," Sage said. "The fango story it is."

But Moxie noticed that Sage hesitated. Perhaps he sensed that Kelso had come near and was listening.

The little heeler grew impatient. "It all began—" she prompted Sage.

"It all began," Sage said slowly. But he hesitated again.

Kelso spoke. "No dog really knows how it began. And no dog knows why the fangos are like they are. Or why—"

" *I* know," old Sage interrupted.

The younger dogs looked back and forth between Sage and Kelso. This was a part of the story they had never heard.

"You are blind," Kelso said.

"I was not blind then."

"Memory fades," said Kelso. "Memory is not history."

"I saw it," Sage said. "I heard it, and I smelled it. I knew the first fango. The first fango was a dog."

"A dog!" The young sheep dogs gasped. "A fango was a dog!"

Kelso barked, "Not true! Not true!" and the younger dogs cowered.

But Sage continued. "Yes, indeed, Kelso. The first fango was a dog. And a hungry dog. We were all hungry dogs. It was in those first bad days after the humans went away. Their buildings became smoke, and they went away. We dogs knew the humans meant to come back to us—"

"And now they have!" a young dog yipped. "At least, one of them has."

"The boy! The boy!" Many young dogs barked.

Moxie looked up to the hilltop where the boy was carrying his sticks.

Sage continued his story. "Now that the boy is here, you all should know the truth. The humans went away, and we dogs kept guarding the sheep. We guarded the sheep although we had nothing to eat. Day after day, in sun and rain, and we had nothing to eat but the grass. Dogs aren't like sheep. We can't live on grass. We dogs were starving. We were wasting away. Then dogs started dying. First some puppies. Then some mothers."

"Puppies! Mothers!" The younger dogs were horrified, but Moxie noticed most of the puppies weren't really listening.

"We grew thinner and thinner," Sage said. "We were desperate. Then one day it happened."

The young dogs all leaned forward.

"One day," Sage told them, "a dog killed a sheep."

A gasp went up from all the young dogs.

"Never!" Kelso barked. "Never! Never! Never!"

Higher in the meadow, Moxie saw the boy turn to see what the commotion was.

Sage shook his shaggy head. "It happened," he said. "It was bound to happen. One day. One dog. He killed one sheep."

Sage paused; then he said, "And then we dogs could eat."

The younger dogs were incredulous. "A dog killed a sheep? How? No sheep dog can kill a sheep—"

"No, he can't!" Kelso yipped. "He can't kill a sheep and remain a sheep dog!"

"We ate," Sage said. "We stayed alive."

"Preposterous!" Kelso barked harshly. "Unbelievable."

And, in fact, the idea of killing a sheep was far beyond most of the younger dogs' imaginations. But Moxie's mind was racing ahead.

"Old Sage," she said. "Brave Kelso, please. How did killing a sheep turn a dog into a fango?"

Kelso growled in a low rumble. "He must have already been a fango, to kill the sheep. A true sheep dog cannot kill sheep."

But Sage was still shaking his head. "No, Kelso. He was indeed a dog. He killed a sheep. We all ate. We survived."

There was silence.

"And then what?" Moxie asked. There was more to know. There had to be.

Sage turned his great head toward her. "And then, Moxie girl? Well, I'll tell you. Then we dogs thought about what had been done. And then what? *We fought about it.* There came a great dog war like you could not believe. Some dogs wanted to kill more sheep. Some dogs said we must stop. Then a few dogs killed another sheep. And they liked killing the sheep. And then they could not stop themselves. In a frenzy, they slaughtered as many sheep as they could. We other dogs fought them, to stop them, to save the sheep. There was an awful, bloody battle."

Sage let the information sink in. "And finally," he said, "in the end? We dogs who would not kill sheep defeated the killer dogs. And we banished those dogs from our pack. We shunned them. And that was when Fango and his followers took to living in the forest."

"Fango?" Moxie asked. "Who is Fango?"

"Fango was the sheep dog who killed the first sheep," said Sage. "We called them all fangos after that." Sage's voice grew quieter. "Fango still lives. Only he and I are old enough to remember the humans and the great war."

Sage was now silent. Kelso growled again. Up on the hillside, the boy piled his sticks.

"But, Sage," Moxie said. "Those dogs were still dogs, weren't they? What turned them into fangos? Was it killing the sheep?"

"No, it was not having humans. A dog is not a dog if he does not have a human. A human is more than a dog's best friend. Without a human to share life with, a dog can lose even his bark."

"But we sheep dogs have been without humans almost forever," said Moxie. "How can we still bark? How can we still be true dogs?"

"A dog's bark, little Moxie, is like the voice of his soul. It's the human part of a dog. So a fango cannot bark. No dog can go wild and ever bark again. We sheep dogs can bark because, in our hearts, we have kept the spirit of the humans. As long as we guard these sheep, we will remain true dogs."

Moxie looked to Kelso, expecting him to argue. But he did not.

"Vigilance," Kelso said. "The word is *vigilance,* whether we have humans or not."

That was good, Moxie thought. But, she wondered, was that all there was—vigilance? Her mind kept working. What was going on here between the sheep dogs and the fangos? Certainly, the sheep dogs kept the fangos from slaughtering all the sheep. But without those fango raids, which drove off some sheep but left others dead and dying, the sheep dogs would have nothing to eat. There was something deep here and perhaps ages old.

Moxie was about to ask her questions, but then one of the pups started barking, probably out of sheer excitement. The little dog barked from the depths of her soul until Moxie and the other younger dogs were compelled to join her. Soon Kelso and Sage were barking, too, and the entire meadow filled with their music. Then, faintly, from the depths of the forest, rose the high, shrill keen of the fangos. Up above the dogs, at the top of the meadow, the boy stopped his stick work and listened.

The other young dogs ran off to play, but Moxie stayed back.

"Old Sage," she said. "I know now where fangos came from. But what about boys? Where do humans come from? How do they think? How do they speak?"

Sage settled back and gave a whispery *Whuf!*

"Ah, Moxie," he said, "I could tell you boy stories all a dog day long, but the fact remains—humans are a mystery. I was taught that dogs tamed the humans many, many years ago. This was back when dogs had not become true yet, and the humans were nothing more than a roving pack of rascals.

"In those days, dogs followed the wild animal herds. Dogs harvested some animals for food, but all was in a balance. Then the humans arrived. They made their living by following the dogs. Whenever the dogs began eating, the humans chased them away and stole the dogs' food."

Moxie imagined the scene as Sage continued. "They were clever—the humans—more clever than dogs. They were also more violent to each other. However, the humans were like dogs in one good way. Human parents loved their children. The human puppies—boys and girls—played and played all day. Their parents let them play. They protected and fed them. But remember, the humans fed them food that they had stolen from the dogs.

"Well, Moxie, the dogs could not let this situation continue. The humans were doing other bad things, too. They were killing many other animals, and the world was getting out of balance. So one day the dogs decided they had to tame the humans. And they sent a brave puppy—a little dog younger than you—to go and live with them. Now, because humans love all children, they loved this puppy, too. They took her in, and they raised her. At first, they fed her food that they had stolen from dogs.

"But together, Moxie, the little dog and the humans discovered many things. They learned to herd animals, rather than just follow them. They became partners, and more than just partners, they became friends. They changed each other's lives.

"So this little dog grew up and she shared the humans' world. In secret, she married a male dog who had stayed with the pack. She had puppies, and they grew up with the humans, too. All true dogs are now descended from that first puppy who went to live with the humans. All of us. What do you think of that?"

"What was her name?" Moxie asked.

"Her name?" Sage said. He thought a moment. "I think that her name was Dog."

Moxie was amazed, but the story seemed right, and she needed to know more. "But Sage, what did the dog learn about the humans? I mean, how do humans—?" But Moxie didn't know how to finish the question.

"Humans are complicated, Moxie. I told you they are a mystery. But here are a few of the things that I know. Humans are clever. They can see very well, and they can put things together to make new things. They change the world everywhere they go. This is why we dogs call them the masters. But it is obvious that their smell sense is very weak, and the way they think and communicate is limited, too—to barking, mainly. For example, sometimes humans think by barking out loud. But I was told that often humans think by barking in their minds. The inside of a human's mind must be a very noisy place."

"I like barking," Moxie said.

"Oh, so do most dogs," said Sage. "But dogs are more complete animals than humans are. Sure, we dogs can bark with our mouths, and we growl. But we don't speak or think in just a mouth-way. We speak and think with our bodies, with our eyes, and with our tails. But we mainly think and speak in smells.

"Moxie," Sage asked. "Do you know why dogs have such long faces?"

"To bite with!" Moxie said.

"Well, yes," Sage said. "But that's not all of it. We dogs have our long faces so we can have long noses to smell with.

"And do you know why our noses are always wet? It's so we can smell with the *outsides* of our noses, too. We use our whole noses, inside and out. We barely have to sniff, and we are reading the news. We know what is happening now and what has happened in the past.

"It's how dogs know a good story. We don't have to ask a friend, 'Hey, Rex, what happened to you?' because as dogs we *smell* what happened to Rex. Whether it was happy or frightening or exciting or disgusting. Or merely embarrassing. We dogs can smell it.

"A smell is evidence. A smell is a memory. A smell is a memory that lasts a long time. Smelling is how we dogs remember and how we think and communicate. Humans may be more clever, but we dogs have more sense."

Moxie had become aware of everything she was smelling at that moment. She smelled Sage, herself, the grass in the sunlight, the grass still in shade, the sunlight itself, and even the path that the boy had walked on, just once, three days before. Moxie realized that part of the reason that she could not understand the boy at first was that the boy's smell was so strange. It was like a whole different language.

Sage and Moxie were quiet together for a time. Then Sage said, "I want to tell you one more thing about dogs and humans. And that is that a human's barking takes time, while a dog's smelling is all at once. A human's story can take hours to tell, and humans must use their cleverness to keep the story going. But a dog's smell-story is just like the memory itself, and every dog can share it, at once and in the same way."

Moxie sniffed, trying to capture all that Sage meant, but it had gotten difficult.

"Smelling is believing," Sage told her. "And we'll have much more to smell before this is over."

21

Over the next few days, Jack went exploring. He searched among the ruins of the house and barn. He made new discoveries every few minutes. He found a pot, a rusty hoe blade, an ax head, some square-headed nails, and a roll of brittle red wire. In a corner of the house ruins, he found a flaky, crumbling mass of what had been spoons and forks, now all rusted together. But he also found a few pieces of real silverware. They were tarnished black, but usable. He thought about how they had once been someone's sparkling pride. With these tools, he reasoned, he could build his new life. They would help keep him alive until he was found. And he *would* be found, Jack tried to persuade himself, now that he could stay alive.

Jack used the hoe blade to dig around in what appeared to be an old garden, searching for root crops that might now be growing wild. He found radishes, potatoes, carrots, and onions. Jack thought of Cookie as he pared the knobby potatoes and tossed them into his pot. He tried to work his eyebrows as Cookie always had. He tried to express surprise, dismay, and delight—all his emotions at once, just like Cookie. Jack laughed. *Life is a scouse!* he thought. Life is a ship's stew, all mixed up.

Jack boiled his stew and tasted it, and then he boiled it some more. He tasted it again. "The carrots," he muttered, as much like Cookie as he could. "The carrots lost their crunch. The potatoes are gummy—but pretty darn good!

"It lacks salt," Jack said louder, to no one around.

He realized that he hadn't found any salt. But then Jack thought of sea salt. He remembered how they evaporated salt in San Francisco Bay. *Of course!* he thought. He could evaporate seawater in rock pockets by the beach.

That is, he thought darkly, if he could get to the beach, past Mr. Bones and the wild dogs. Jack began to feel helpless again. He searched out the old blind sheep dog and sat by him for a while, hoping to soak up some wisdom.

22

Days passed. Moxie watched the boy as he watched the water and the forest and he piled more sticks. He was growing more restless. Sometimes he barked softly to himself. Then he got quiet and stared at the forest. Then he shook his head and waved his forelegs and gathered more sticks.

Finally Jack thought he had enough courage. He left the old farmstead and walked down through the meadow. He began exploring the edge of it, where the forest began. The little Border collie came following along.

They trailed down along the woods to the meadow's far corner. There, Jack found them—the apple trees. This area had once been the orchard. Now it was being overgrown, reclaimed by the forest, but Jack could see a man-made pattern—the regular spacing of the apple trees.

"This is good," he said.

The apples were green yet, but Jack picked one down from a tree. He bit into it. It was tart but exciting.

He turned to the little Border collie. "Here, girl!" he said. "Want a bite of an apple?"

He squatted down and held the bitten apple out to her. She slowly began to creep toward him. Jack smiled. She might be beginning to trust him.

Jack cooed to her, "Here, girl. Here. Come on. Try the apple."

The little dog came closer and raised her nose to the apple. Slowly, slowly, with her whole body quivering and one front paw held up off the ground, the little dog touched her nose to the fruit.

Then she stiffened, and her eyes jerked to the side. It was funny, but Jack tried not to laugh. Then out of the corner of his eye, to his right, he caught the slow movement of a shadow.

Now Jack froze. Neither he nor the little dog moved for as long as they could hold their breaths. Then both of them slowly turned their heads, and they saw that the shadow had eyes. Yellow stone eyes. *Oh, no,* Jack thought. Then the shadow stepped forward, and it wasn't a shadow anymore. It was Mr. Bones. The hair on Jack's neck rose. The little Border collie quailed. Mr. Bones curled back his lips and showed his yellow, broken teeth.

Jack heard another sound. He looked left. Two more wild dogs stood in the shadows by tree trunks. Jack heard a dry rustling—behind him—but he feared to turn his head to see what it was.

Jack glanced down. On the ground, between him and the little dog, lay a three-foot-long broken apple tree branch. He heard the rustling again behind him—closer now—and the skin on his back twitched like it was crawling. Somehow, from his last experience with them, Jack felt that the creatures would not attack until they got really close or until he started running. His mind raced to form a plan. He would reach down and grab the branch and swing it around and hope that it hit something. In front of him, the little dog was wide-eyed and trembling, looking behind him. Jack peered into her eyes, hoping to see a reflection. He listened intently, trying to judge how close the danger was. He waited, tense and quivering.

Then right behind him Jack heard a *pop!* The little dog whimpered. Jack reached down, grabbed the branch, swung it around, and caught one of the beasts squarely on the side of its head. The impact knocked Jack onto his behind, but he scrambled backward and jumped up. He looked left and right. The other wild dogs had not moved. The one that he had just smashed with the branch lay on its side in the litter of leaves, just beginning to raise its head from the ground.

With the creatures watching Jack and him watching them, Jack slowly backed up into the meadow until he could see them no more. They did not follow him, and Jack realized that they probably did not go into the open in the daytime. They were not cowards—just careful killers.

Then Jack remembered the little dog was still in there, in the old orchard with the killers.

"Hey! Hey!" he shouted, and he ran back down to the edge of the woods.

But the Border collie and all of the wild dogs had vanished. Jack walked back and forth along the front line of trees.

"Hey! Little dog!" he called frantically. But he could not make himself go back into the forest.

24

Protect the boy, Moxie had been thinking. *Protect the boy.* But she was frozen with fear.

Then the boy had swung around and hit one fango with the tree limb. The boy fell down, but he got up again. He backed away toward the meadow and disappeared behind branches and leaves.

That stirred Moxie. She started to follow the boy, but a fango stepped into her path. The fango lowered his head and bared his teeth.

Moxie looked left and right. There were fangos all around. It was only behind her, toward the deeper forest, that there was a small gap in the fangos' line. Moxie moved fast. She spun in a quick circle and sprinted through the gap, intent on getting around the fangos' flank.

But she could not get around them. As she circled back toward the meadow, she met another fango, then another, and another again. Each time she changed direction, another fango appeared in her way. Everywhere, Moxie was thwarted and blocked, and she was pushed back farther from the meadow. Moxie ran hard. Her breath burned her throat. Her heart hammered her ribs. But at every turn, the creatures turned her deeper into the forest. The fangos were herding her, like a sheep they had stolen from the flock.

Soon Moxie found herself in a dark, tree-lined arena, strewn all about with bleaching sheep bones. She dashed to the middle of it and whirled around. She snarled, but she was shaking with fear.

The fangos were already there, all around the arena's edges.

Soon the fango leader stepped into the clearing. The creature was old. He looked older than Sage. But where Sage's coat was lustrous and thick, the fango leader's scabrous skin stretched over his ribs. He slowly padded up to Moxie and settled back on his haunches.

He did not set his eyes on her at first, but even his scent was terrifying. He reeked of dead meat, of putrid mutton. Worse, he smelled of dead dog flesh, too. Moxie fought for breath. She got set again to run. But the leader fango spoke.

"Mm—mm—me, mmm, Fango—" he said in a hoarse, soggy growl.

Moxie started. This was Fango himself! This was Fango, the dog who—according to Sage—had killed the first sheep.

Fango appeared frustrated. He worked his jaws, as though trying to bark.

"Y—yoo—you—" Fango said. Or he said something close to it.

"Yoo—" he said again. It was not quite a bark, not quite a word. "Yoo—dorg—uh, uh. You, dorg—"

Dog? Was that what he said? You, dog? Moxie glanced around to check the other fangos. They were slowly approaching.

"You, dorg," Fango said to Moxie again. His manner was ugly, but he seemed to be trying to connect.

Moxie nodded jerkily. Her fear made it hard for her to speak. "Me, dog," she said. "I am a dog."

Fango nodded now, and he exhaled a nauseating stench. He worked his jaws and tried again to speak.

"—Y-y-yoo-mun," he managed.

"You mean 'human?'" Moxie said.

Fango's eyes widened. "Yuh!" he said. "Yuh, huh." He nodded. He looked around at his followers. They were now only a few yards away.

"Yoomun!" he said to the other fangos. This word excited Fango, but the other fangos' eyes stayed dull and hungry.

Yoomun? Moxie wondered. She thought he might be

talking about the boy. But was it for a good reason or a bad one?

"Human?" she said to Fango. "Human. Boy?"

Fango nodded. "B-b-b-b—" he attempted, but he could not say the simple word.

At that moment one of the other fangos stepped even closer. Fango spun toward him and snarled.

"B-b-b-b—!" he stammered at all of the fangos. "B-b-b-b—!"

But they showed no understanding, nor any desire to understand. Instead, they looked dully and hungrily at Moxie, who crouched even lower, ready to run. And then one fango, then another, stepped closer.

Fango rumbled a low growl at them, and they stopped. Then Fango closed his eyes. He tried again to speak to Moxie.

"B-b-b-b—b-b-b-b—" he tried, but he could not say it. "B-b-b-b—b-b-b-b—" Then his eyes snapped open. They drilled into Moxie's eyes with anger and frustration.

"B-b-b-b—B-b-b-b—" he tried again, and Moxie realized that while old Sage may have lost sight, Fango had lost something far more important. He had lost language. The way he smelled, the way he moved—it all gave Moxie the sense that Fango had lost his very soul. He was a killer. That was all. Fango was no longer a dog. And the boy, Moxie now thought, was an unbearable reminder of what Fango used to be—and could never be again.

"B-b-b-b—B-b-b-b—" Fango kept stammering, and Moxie felt her courage grow.

"Boy!" Moxie barked. "Boy! Boy!"

Fango jerked at the sense of the word.

"Boy! Boy!" Moxie barked.

Fango staggered. Then he nodded. He looked again at Moxie with a regard of absolute loss.

"Boy!" Moxie barked, in growing defiance. She swallowed back the pity that any true dog would feel.

"Boy!" she hurled at him.

Fango's eyes flared.

Then a grating growl came from the side.

Moxie looked. Another fango had stepped even closer.

Fango snarled at him. But Fango's followers weren't listening. They were closing in on Moxie.

Then Moxie felt a low, buzzing rumble. She looked at Fango and realized the vibration was coming from him. Then she heard it. Fango was growling. The rumble grew into thunder.

"Arrr-ghhh!" Fango roared, and he launched himself at the closest creature. A vicious, roaring fight erupted all around.

Moxie ducked and watched as Fango raged. Fur and slaver

flew, and so did bodies. That small part of Fango that re-membered being a dog was undeniably gone.

Moxie saw her chance and bolted. She ran all out through the forest and burst into the meadow. She ran straight past the boy.

25

After the encounter with the wild dogs in the old orchard, Jack kept to the meadow. Days passed, but he did not count them. He thought about how time itself seemed to have changed. A day could seem like an entire season. Could a season feel like just one day? He had been sure that he would spy a sail and light his fire and then be saved. But he hadn't seen a single ship, and time passed, day after day. Jack began to think that ships were avoiding the island, probably because of the rocks and the currents. And perhaps because there were no reasons to come to it. After all, it had no people. So Jack stopped spending so much time at the top of the sea-cliff. He checked for sails now only a few times a day. He scoured the meadow's edges for more wood for his camp and the signal fire, but was afraid to venture into the forest or back down to the beach. He had not yet made the sea salt he wanted, although he could remember Cookie telling him that his body needed salt.

Jack built things in the meadow. He built a rude shelter from some square stones. But at night the shelter was cold and dank and very small. Jack couldn't stand sleeping in it, unless it was rainy and he couldn't sleep under the stars. So he built a circular stone windbreak for his fire. He often sat and dozed in the face of the fire's warmth, and he dreamed of the *Patty B* and San Francisco. Sometimes he'd wake, certain he was smelling Cookie's coffee, but it was only his own shorts beginning to singe near the fire.

During the days, when Jack didn't need heat, he buried the coals. This kept the fire going at a slow, smokeless punk. He looked for more projects. He improved the meadow's spring by building a small rock dam so the water would pool. He bathed in the cold water, scrubbing himself with tough, scratchy leaves. Then he stripped the bark from some saplings and fashioned a pipe from the bark for the water to pour through. Many of the dogs drank from the pipe. They seemed to like the novelty. Jack liked the sound of the water.

Jack realized he might have to plant a crop before long, so he dug a root cellar to store his vegetables. It was not a cellar so much as a little cave with some shelves made from rocks and sticks. He also saw that he would need more clothes. His shirt and shorts weren't enough to cover him, and they were becoming tattered and torn.

Jack's nerves were slowly fraying, too. And it was all because of the slow business of survival. Jack thought that survival was OK, as far as it went. Scavenging was more interesting when his stomach was empty. But when Jack's stomach started to feel half full instead of half empty, the whole staying-alive job began to feel much like a chore. Survival was fine, but Jack needed something more.

The dogs were fine, too, but he longed for conversation. And these dogs still had not warmed to Jack in the way he wanted them to. The younger dogs chased his sticks, but then played keep-away with each other. The older dogs still shooed the puppies away. And the big leader dog, the German shepherd, seemed not to trust Jack. Why not? The little black-and-white Border collie appeared to be almost obsessed with Jack, but even she kept at a distance. If only he could bridge the gap.

About a week later, in the middle of the night, Jack half-woke beside his dying fire. He grabbed a piece of wood and leaned forward to toss it onto the coals. But then he noticed an odor that made the corners of his mouth turn down. It was an awful smell. He leaned back, meaning to look around, and he felt a cold, dry nose touch the base of his neck.

"Aaah!" Jack twisted around so fast that his spine popped. He scuttled backward, crouching low, on his hands and feet. Breathless, heart pounding, he peered past the fire into the darkness, and he saw two small bright orange sparks that were eyes.

Jack stood and raised the stick of firewood.

The two orange eyes moved closer, and Mr. Bones stepped into the fire's light.

"Oh—you," Jack said in a hoarse whisper.

The dire creature appeared to be examining Jack. For a long minute, the wild dogs' leader took in Jack's stock and measure. Then he turned and padded silently away, a yellowish shadow joining the blackness.

Jack shuddered. Then he shook harder. He rubbed his neck where he had been touched. He mounded wood on the fire and made it flare up. He shuddered again as he wondered whether the wild dog had intended to attack—or instead had meant merely to touch him.

26

Time passed. One day Jack found a piece of a broken mirror in the rubble of the ruins. He took it down through the meadow and washed it in the spring. When he looked at himself in it, he was amazed. His face was tanned dark. His eyes were wide and wild. His hair, which he had not combed in all this time, had grown long. It was dirty and frizzy, sticking out in all directions.

"Who is this?" he said. He looked at himself and smiled. He thought that he looked like Toa and Tanati.

"Sabbee, Jack," he said to himself, remembering how the twins used to tell him to understand.

"Sabbee, Jack," he said to himself. "You will float."

A memory of the storm made him feel sad. Jack stared at

himself in the mirror shard for a long time. Then he put it away in the tobacco tin. He walked to the cliff-top and checked the ocean for sails. Then he went back down to the wall and got out the mirror again. He took it to his campfire and pulled out a half-burnt twig. Then he—carefully, carefully—drew on his face the most intricate lines. He drew line after line, and line upon line, until his whole face was covered.

Jack liked what he saw. *There,* he thought. *There!* He looked like a Maori, fierce and tattooed.

27

The boy's new face surprised Moxie, but she got used to it. To her, the lines looked like hair. She liked it more when he drew hairlines on his shoulders. He was beginning to look more like a dog.

But the moment she realized this, it bothered her. She did not want a dog. She wanted a boy. She had felt shame since she'd failed to protect the boy from the fangos. She wanted another chance to act like a dog and to protect the boy or save him.

More days passed, and Jack drew more tattoos. He didn't draw pictures, just lines and points. And waves and zigzags. They were handsome, he thought. He got pretty good at it. But still, he began to grow more uneasy. He made a joke— what would he do when he ran out of skin? But he didn't laugh, because it wasn't a good joke. And he was restless. He wasn't bored, because one has to be comfortable to really be bored. But he was restless and twitchy.

That is it, he thought, and he almost said it aloud—*I need some adventure.* But he knew in his heart that he had had plenty of adventure. What was wrong was that most of the action had happened *to* him. He had not planned it, and he had not caused it, and he had no one to share it with. Jack was stranded on the island and trapped in the meadow, living with sheep dogs he could not quite figure out. He had not gone to the beach because of the wild dogs. He had not explored the forest for the same reason. But since Jack had come to the island, several sheep had been killed by the wild dogs, and other sheep may have been rustled. Jack now found himself watching the woods for signs of the murderous forest thugs, almost wishing for an attack.

And then one came. It was near dusk. The forest was dark. Jack happened to be high on the meadow, and he saw it all. The moon was just rising, and Jack was watching it when a squad of wild dogs slipped out of the forest and surrounded a sheep that had strayed from the flock. The sheep panicked, darting this way and that. But the wild dogs used their herding skills, and they hit and bit at the sheep and got it moving toward the forest. Then one of the sheep dog sentries spotted them and sent up a howl.

Immediately, the German shepherd and three other big males were bounding to the rescue. Five of the wild dogs wheeled around to face the four sheep dogs. The big shepherd slammed into one of them and knocked him to the ground. A snarling, whirling fight ensued. Jack stood and watched, entranced by the mayhem.

Then the battle was over. The wild dogs were gone. Jack

felt flushed with energy, as though he had fought them himself. He ran down to look at the sheep, and he found it was dead. Its windpipe had been torn out, like a hose. Somehow Jack had missed seeing it actually happen, but the wild dogs had killed the sheep before they retreated. Jack wondered why. Maybe for practice, he thought. Now the sheep dogs all gathered around the dead sheep. Everything was quiet. The night was getting darker.

With the big German shepherd watching the woods, three big sheep dogs dragged the dead sheep up the hill toward Jack's camp, to a place they could defend against another attack. Then the German shepherd approached the dead sheep, and he tore out a chunk of meat for himself. Then he stood back, and the new and pregnant mothers came forward. They tore away meat for themselves and their puppies. Then the other dogs took their portions. There was some sharp snarling and snapping among the sheep dogs, but all in all Jack was impressed by the polite order of the banquet.

The sheep dogs worked at the sheep's carcass from the inside out. The fleece stayed intact, and Jack got the idea that he might make himself something out of it. He found his knife and approached the dead sheep. A few dogs growled at him, but none physically challenged him. So Jack grabbed the sheep and rolled it over onto its back.

First, Jack carved himself some mutton and took that to his root cellar to keep it safe. Then he returned, and he cut the sheep's fleece off the carcass. He intended to make himself some clothing. Jack wasn't sure how, but he figured he had to scrape all the flesh from the hide and then do something to keep the hide from getting stiff. He dragged the fleece over by his campfire and used the hoe blade and knife to do the scraping. This was simple enough, but it took all night. Then Jack pounded the inside of the hide with a big rock.

When the skin began to dry, he took it down to the spring pool, and he soaked it. He had heard Father Maley once say that the American Indians did that. The Indians also boiled hides, Jack thought, with bark or something. They boiled hides and tanned them into leather. But his pot wasn't big enough to boil a sheep's fleece. So he decided to smoke it, although he didn't know if the Indians did that. Jack piled green branches onto his campfire and hung the fleece on poles laid across his stone windbreak. He let the heavy smoke soak into the fleece. Then he took the fleece down and soaked it again and pounded it more, and then he smoked it again. He did this for the entire day.

And success! It was ugly, but the fleece was soft enough to work now. Jack was proud. He cut holes in the fleece for his head and his arms. This way he made a long cape. It hung down his back to his calves. It was very impressive. He showed it off to the sheep dogs. They shied away from it.

"OK," he said. "So it's ugly."

It was also heavy and uncomfortable. It itched.

And soon Jack noticed that it stank.

By the following day, it reeked. It smelled of smoke and gore and rot. It soon stank so bad that Jack couldn't bear to wear it. He took it off and threw it away from his camp. He took time to roast a small meal of potatoes, but he smelled the stink on his hands and it nauseated him. He took a bath in the spring pool and scrubbed himself with rough leaves, but he could not get the horrible smell off his skin or out of his hands. The tattoos were coming off, but the odor remained.

As Jack scrubbed at his hands, he began to worry. Was this permanent? What if he could never get away from his own stench? It was driving him crazy. Finally, he ran to the cliff tops and stood facing the breeze and gulping fresh air. The slow despair of survival returned to him, but it was deeper now. Jack was alone. And he was stinking up the world. All Jack could think was, *What? What! What!* He was losing all his words.

"What! What! What!" he shouted. "WHAT! WHAT! WHAT?"

What? Was he scared? Was he mad? He didn't know. He

looked around. He was standing on the headland at the island's highest point, next to his woodpile for a signal fire. The ocean foam swirled far below him. A seagull flew between Jack and the foam and then banked toward the mainland, free. Jack cursed and kicked a piece of wood off the cliff. It fell twirling to the narrow beach. Jack watched it fall.

Then Jack kicked another piece off, and he watched that fall, too. Then he picked up a big, long stick, and he hurled it out, as far as he could. And that did it. For a brief moment, Jack felt like leaping from the cliff and following the stick down. Instead, with a mighty shove, he pushed the entire woodpile off the cliff. In his hurry, he tripped. He almost *did* follow the wood over the cliff. He lay on his stomach and watched the wood clatter down to the narrow beach. The sticks and logs and branches that he had so patiently gathered all fell tumbling down the cliff.

Jack lay in his despair, and he watched all his work fall. Several of the bigger sticks bounced out into the water. The rip current caught them and carried them away. The sticks bounced in the fast flow, and they spun.

Jack watched until he lost sight of the sticks. He jumped to his feet, but they were gone.

"They are *going* somewhere!" he exclaimed.

He felt a sudden compelling impulse to follow.

Moxie watched the boy. What was he doing now? Humans loved sticks, so why was he pushing them all off the cliff? Was this a game? It didn't look like the boy was having fun. Now he was just lying on his stomach, looking down off the cliff.

Then the boy jumped up. He stood still, looking down at the ocean. Then suddenly the boy turned and began running. He ran past Moxie to the old ruins and his camp. He rummaged around until he found a coil of something and grabbed it. Then he began running again, straight for the fango forest.

What was this? What was he doing? Moxie ran after him. Where was he going?

At the same time, Jack felt both free and compelled. He ran down through the woods without seeing a wild dog. He carried the roll of wire he had taken from his supplies. He burst out onto the beach and ran along it to the cliffs. There he found his firewood, broken and scattered. He began gathering the longer pieces and piling them together, side by side. He worked at it until he had a bundle of sticks about two feet thick and six feet long. It wasn't pretty, he thought, but it would have to do. He fashioned lengths of wire by rapidly bending the wire back and forth until it broke and used these to tie up the bundle of sticks.

Jack felt even more certain of his decision, now that he had made his raft. It didn't look like a raft. It was just an ugly bundle. But the sticks were too skinny and irregular to tie together any other way, and Jack was in a hurry. He wanted to get onto his raft and out into the current quickly, before he could change his mind. He tried not to think about how dangerous and foolhardy his plan was. The current would take him where it had taken the *Patty B*—on to safety or to its wreckage.

Jack rolled the bundle out into the light surf, and he floated it out through the breakers. He clambered on top of it, but it rolled over and dumped him. Jack waited a moment, to see in which position the raft floated naturally, and then he climbed on the raft again, this time from its end.

He lay on his chest and started paddling with his hands, as he had seen the Maoris and Owyhee Islanders do on their surfing boards. He paddled out into the current. He felt the rip current catch him, and he felt his raft speed up. His heartbeat and his breathing and his spirit accelerated. He was on his way now, to wherever he was going.

31

Moxie dashed back and forth along the water's edge. Where was the boy going? Was he going away? He had rolled his stick bundle into the ocean and crawled on top of it. He had rolled off; then he climbed back on again. He started paddling away.

Moxie dashed into the surf, then out, then in again. She could not help herself. The boy! The boy! She had to follow him. Suddenly, she was in past the breakers, and the current had her. She could not see the boy. She could not see the shore. She saw only the sky and the splashing waves.

32

The current swept Jack past one of the great leaning rocks and an eddy-whirl spun his small craft around. He was moving backward now in the current's vast power. It thrilled him. It frightened him. He felt—here we go now!

And then in the water behind his raft Jack saw something swimming. It was a shark! No. A sea lion?

No.

It was the black-and-white Border collie. She was twenty yards behind him, paddling for all she was worth, and that wasn't nearly enough. Her nose stuck straight up in the air. Her front paws slapped the water. She, too, was caught in the current's power, spinning in hopeless circles.

Jack began to paddle back against the current, toward the

little dog. But as they both sped along, she remained far away from him. He looked back over his shoulder, in the direction they were going, and saw trouble coming up fast.

One of the great leaning rocks lay dead ahead. The current hit it and split in two. Half of the current poured between the rock and the island's cliffs. The other half flowed more slowly out into the ocean. That way was obviously the safe way to go. Jack worked to turn his raft away from the island, and he started to paddle again, but he looked back once more at the little dog. She was still caught like a leaf in the rushing current. And she was lower in the water. She was losing her strength.

Jack looked back at the leaning rock. He had one last chance to miss going between it and the cliff. He pulled mightily with both arms, but the current had him. It sucked his raft backward and slammed it against the rock.

The raft exploded into sticks and splinters. Jack plunged beneath the waves. He fought his way to the surface, but the current slammed him against the rock. He spun, bouncing along the rock where the current was slowed by the friction. Out in midcurrent, the little dog had almost caught up to him. Only the tip of her nose now showed above the water. As she neared him, Jack drew up both his feet as far as he could and then pushed off mightily from the rock wall.

This propelled him out into the faster flow, and there he was now, right next to the little dog. As she spun in front of him, he grabbed her hind leg and then wrapped one arm around her chest.

Swimming with one arm and kicking hard with his legs, Jack stayed afloat as the current spit them out at the far end of the strait. The current here slowed and became a train of big waves. There was another narrow beach just ahead.

With slow strokes, Jack was able to swim to the beach. He crawled ashore and fell onto the sand, letting go of the little dog. She jumped up and, without looking back, ran away from him up the hillside.

Moxie ran as fast as her exhausted legs would carry her, all the way up through the woods and into the meadow. When she got to the ruins, she collapsed in her confusion. All she could think was *What was all that about?*

Why did the boy go into the sea? Why did I follow him?

Why did he grab me?

Why did I run?

34

Jack had never felt worse. He could not have hurt more. He realized that his body now hurt the way his heart had been aching. He felt physically the way he had felt in his spirit. He lay for the rest of the day on the beach, in the sun, feeling hopeless. Then as the sun lowered, he remembered the wild dogs. And then there came that instinct again, that nagging sense for survival. It was dull at first, but still it made him stand up and take a stout stick for protection on his way back up to the meadow.

As Jack walked through the dread forest, he felt another sensation. This one almost felt good. What was it? Was it his own courage? With his stick held ready, he began to feel a small spark of bravery. If courage is what it was, then courage felt tired, but good.

Then behind Jack a twig snapped, and he panicked and ran. He didn't look back until he was well up into the meadow and his courage was far behind.

Another day passed. Or was it ten days? Jack spent most of his time now beside his campfire. He tried to doze. He tried to daydream. He tried to pass the time without thinking about how time was passing.

But he knew it was. Time was passing Jack by. He began to think of himself less as a castaway and more as a prisoner. He was a prisoner of the island. He was a prisoner of the wild dogs. In some ways, he was a prisoner of the sheep dogs, too. And the sheep dogs, he realized, were themselves prisoners—of their strange situation on the island. Jack had not seen the sheep dogs themselves kill a sheep yet. It was as though they depended on the evil wild dogs to do their dirty work—if dirty work was what it was. Perhaps the sheep dogs didn't know what was happening, but it was a weird and uncomfortable state of balance. Perhaps the sheep dogs and the wild dogs relied on each other. If so, it could go on forever.

Forever was a word that kept creeping into Jack's mind. The way his body ached after his attempted escape let him imagine what it felt like to grow old. And that reminded Jack of old Father Maley and how he had read to the orphan boys about island castaways, marooned like the clever Robinson Crusoe, or poor Ben Gunn in *Treasure Island*. What Jack remembered about the stories was how *old* the castaways were. They grew beards. They grew strange. They were like prisoners of a time that had stranded them on their islands, but all the while—like the ocean current—*real* time was still flowing by them.

Jack shook his head when he got to thinking like that. He resisted it by dreaming deep into his past. He worked up dozing daydreams of being a boy in his parents' home and of being the ship's boy on the *Patty B.* He tried harder than ever to make friends with the dogs. He threw sticks for them until he was exhausted. *Somehow,* he thought, *I've got to stay a boy.* It was more important than surviving.

Jack worked at his dreams. But there was one particular dream that always got to him.

36

Jack dreamed he was back in the St. Brendan orphanage. A knock came at the door, and the door opened. And standing there were an old sailor and a boy. The way the old sailor's pipe smoke drifted around them, they were both almost impossible to see.

"WELL?" Father Maley shouted, as the sailor's smoke drifted around. Then the old sailor disappeared like a ghost into the smoke, and Father Maley brought in the new boy.

The boy was small—but, of course, all the orphans were small—and Jack could not tell his age or even focus on his face. The boy did not speak, but that was no large matter at St. Brendan's. And so nothing different—well, nothing very different—stood out about this new boy.

Yet there he was, in his way remarkable. It was the sense of him—ardent, fearful, and friendly. It was clear to all of the orphans that he was an orphan, too.

The boy wore sailor's clothes cut down to his size—a gray oiled sweater and a thick black Mackintosh sea coat. The boys at St. Brendan's wore sea outfits also, but their uniforms were fakes, manufactured from bad cotton. They had limp little flaps on the backs of their collars with poorly stitched anchor insignia. The anchors were meant to charm the charity out of rich folk.

The old orphans circled the new orphan, the better to see him and to smell his smell, which now filled the parlor. The boy had that oily, wet, woolly smell of wet sheep, the wet sea, wet dogs, and sleep. When Jack smelled that smell, from somewhere dogs began howling.

Father Maley now shouted above the howling.

"HE IS THE SOLE SURVIVOR!" he shouted.

"OF A TERRIBLE SHIPWRECK!" he yelled.

"ON A SOUTH PACIFIC ISLAND!" he bellowed.

"OFF NEW ZEALAND!" he roared.

"WHERE ALL HANDS!" he thundered. "WERE LOST!

"EXCEPT—!" Father Maley hesitated. The dogs howled, and he shouted louder.

"EXCEPT FOR OUR—!" He took a big breath. "BRAVE NEW BOY!"

Then poor Father Maley began to run out of air.

"He lived ALONE!" he panted. "On a deserted IS-LAND! For how LONG? Well, he SURVIVED!"

The dogs howled, Father Maley gasped, and so did a few of the boys.

"And on WHAT?" he asked them, "did he survive? On PLUCK! On LUCK! And on his WITS!"

Father Maley was staggering. "His PLUCK was ENOUGH!" he rasped. "His LUCK was a MIRACLE! But his WITS? HIS WITS? ALAS! ALACK!"

Father Maley started hacking—barking, really. He collapsed into a chair. He held his hands up in the air. He was wheezing now, and his voice got smaller. "His—wits—!" He was whispering, or whimpering. "May have been—!" He was coughing. "All—used—up—!"

Then Father Maley disappeared into the howling of the dogs, and Jack awoke—*howling.*

Jack threw his hand across his mouth. All was silent. He jumped to his feet. He shook his head, and he slapped his own face. He had just dreamed of himself, seeing himself. And Cookie. And Father Maley. And then all the dogs howling! What was this? Was he falling to pieces? Was he finally coming undone?

He looked around frantically, at the meadow and the sheep and the dogs. It was a gray day. It was drizzling. The little black-and-white Border collie was watching him quizzically.

He shouted at her. "What? What can I do?"

Jack could think of nothing to do but to start gathering wood for another signal fire. Some ship would come by someday. Someday he might be saved.

37

These building-the-stick-pile days were excruciating for Moxie. Now more than ever, the boy enthralled her. Watching him work made her want to work with him. Watching him watch the sea made her watch the sea, too. But she could not break through her embarrassment and let herself go up to him. Twice now, she had not been able to protect or save him.

The other young dogs frolicked and played at a safe distance from the boy, but Moxie wanted to become a real part of what he was. He was a boy. A human boy. He fascinated her. He enchanted her. Whenever he stopped working to whistle to her, it almost drove her crazy to resist it. But even when he whistled, she could not approach him. Shame was that strong inside her.

Kelso said to her, "It's good to see you keeping your distance. Be a true dog. Be vigilant."

"But what is a true dog?" old Sage asked her.

What was a true dog? Moxie did not know. Ever since she had run when the fangos had surrounded her and the boy, she had felt more like a sheep than a dog. And ever since she had run from him after the time in the ocean, she had felt shamed.

It was now a late afternoon above the meadow. Moxie sat at the edge of the sea-cliff and watched the boy walk around his pile of sticks. She thought how right Sage had been when he said, "Humans love sticks." The boy had built a towering pile of them.

It was then that she saw it.

It was there, out on the ocean.

It was a big thing, far out. A black-and-white big thing, moving along far out on the waves. The thing had a black bottom part to it, which slid through the water. And it had a lot of white on top. There were squares of white rising above its black bottom part, and they looked like they were filled with the wind. Moxie had seen these things before. They had sometimes floated past the sheep dogs' island, out on the blue ocean, and then they were gone.

But now this one seemed to be stopping. Moxie barked at

it once. She looked to the boy, but the boy hadn't seen it. He kept walking around his stick pile. Every time he circled it, he stopped and stared down toward the dark forest.

At last the boy stopped for a long while, and he watched the forest, deep in his thinking. Then suddenly he slapped his forepaws together and started walking down through the sheep, striding with his long forelegs swinging at his sides.

Moxie had never seen the boy move with such shoulders-forward purpose, even that time when he went into the ocean. He now strode through the meadow until he came to the edge of the forest. Then, without stopping, the boy marched right into the forest and disappeared.

Moxie stood. What was this? This was dangerous, this was. What was the boy doing? The fangos! This was danger! Moxie stamped her feet and looked around at the other dogs. Most were guarding the sheep or lolling or sleeping. All were unmindful of what the boy had done. Moxie barked at them but got no reaction.

Moxie barked again. The other dogs did nothing. She barked, and she spun around in anxious, tight dread, and she looked all about for help.

The boy was gone! Moxie spun around twice. Her heart shook inside her chest. Her feet stamped the ground by themselves. She spun around again, and then she began to run as fast as she could, down through the meadow toward the dark forest. She was angry with herself. She should never have let the boy out of her sight.

Jack had advanced some twenty yards inside the forest and now stood scanning the trees for signs of the wild dogs. There was more firewood, deeper in. He could see the bleached branches lying on the ground. He needed to get them to build his second woodpile. But his courage had melted and drained away as soon as he had entered the forest.

Jack glanced back behind him, to make sure he had a clear path if he had to run, and it was then that he saw the little black-and-white dog. She was tearing down through the meadow, leaping tussocks and hummocks. She ran hell-bent-for-leather, straight toward Jack. The little dog closed the distance quickly, and she burst full tilt into the forest.

Jack stepped back behind a tree trunk. The little dog

dashed right past him. Then she stopped, another five yards in. She stood with her nose up, stamping her paws, and frantically scanning the forest in front of her. Jack knew she was looking for him.

It made him smile. It made him happy to see how this little dog cared for him. She was so anxious and nervous that it almost made him laugh.

But instead, he watched her. It filled him with joy.

"Boo—!" he said softly, and the little dog spun around.

"Hi," Jack said, and she saw him. They looked at each other for a moment. Then Jack put out his hands, and the little dog ran to him and she jumped into his arms.

Oh! Yes! She was with him now. She covered his face with licking kisses. She whimpered, and she trembled in his arms, and he hugged her as close as he could.

"Hey, girl! Hey, girl!" Jack kept saying. "Hey. You have really got some moxie." He set her down on the ground, and she squirmed and rubbed her side against his legs.

Jack kept laughing. "OK! OK!" And then he got quiet. "Well, OK, then. And what will I call you?"

Jack looked at her. She cocked her head and stared at him intently. The word *moxie* jumped into his brain.

"It's Moxie for you, then," he said. "I'll call you Moxie." He petted the little dog. "My name is Jack. It's Jack," he said. "Jack." Saying his name made him feel even better. He rubbed both Moxie's sides hard with the flats of his hands as she looked up at him, happy, her little tail wagging.

"We're a pair, Moxie," Jack said. "Whatever happens. We're together."

Then Jack looked up into the forest.

"C'mon, Moxie," he said. "Let's gather us up a great bonfire."

He tried to train Moxie to help him gather sticks, but it did not work out quite as he'd hoped it would. Moxie brought him sticks, all right, but often these were the same sticks that Jack had just put onto the pile.

Jack tried to tell her that he wanted the sticks to "stay" on the pile, but then Moxie seemed to think he wanted her to "stay the pile," in the same way she would stay a group of sheep. She stood facing the pile with her head down and her eyes intense, looking as though she was trying to hypnotize the sticks into not moving.

"Oh, what the heck," Jack said. "We're together."

They ended up playing fetch-the-stick and hide-the-stick in the forest. Jack shouted, and Moxie barked, and they ran through the trees. By the time they understood that they were in trouble, it was getting very near dark.

The two of them were standing together, breathing hard,

and Jack was bent over with his hands on his knees, when they saw the shadow that became Mr. Bones.

And then the other wild dogs suddenly appeared in the thick of the forest and the gathering gloom. Just like the earlier times, the wild dogs did not move at first. They just appeared, and they stood, or they sat, and they watched Jack and Moxie.

Jack turned slowly around and saw that they were surrounded. Mr. Bones already stood between them and the meadow.

"Mr. Bones—" Jack whispered.

The old dog's lips pulled back and bared his broken yellow teeth. Jack was holding a stick. He threw it, but it missed and Mr. Bones did not have to budge.

At Jack's side, Moxie growled. Jack turned to look back into the forest. The other wild dogs had moved closer. More had joined them, between and behind trees. Moxie growled again. Jack looked back toward the meadow.

Mr. Bones was now joined by two others. They were closer, too. They panted with their tongues partly out of their mouths in a way that made them look cruel and casual at the same time. Their yellow eyes were empty and deep and hungry.

Only Mr. Bones' eyes held more than an empty evil. He

appeared to be deeply intent on Jack. Then his rib cage swelled, and he began to moan, in an ugly, whiney groan that didn't sound doglike. It sounded almost human, and it made Jack's back crawl.

Moxie growled back at Mr. Bones.

"OK, girl," Jack said to Moxie. "OK—now." But he could think of nothing else to say.

Beside him, Moxie growled lower. The wild dogs and the darkness were closing in.

And fear was already there. It felt like a hole in Jack's stomach and a quivering weakness just above his knees. Jack's breath came quick and short. He felt like he was going to fall down if he did not do something, now.

There was a pile of gathered firewood a few feet away. Jack edged over to it. He reached down slowly and picked up a large, straight limb. The limb was about the size of a base-ball bat, but half again longer. Jack waved it above his head, and he made a step toward Mr. Bones. Mr. Bones did not move.

Jack undid his belt buckle and slid it out of the belt loops. He then made another loop with the belt itself, and he put it around the limb and tightened it so that it would not slip off.

"OK, Moxie," Jack said. He held the end of the belt, and he began to swing the heavy limb around his head.

"Back!" he shouted at Mr. Bones. Jack was trying to threaten, but his voice cracked and shook. "Back!" he shouted again. He took a step toward the meadow. The limb made a low *whoo-whoo* sound as it swung through the air.

"Back!" Jack shouted. "Back!" The arc of the swinging limb moved closer to Mr. Bones' head.

"Back!" Jack shouted. And just before the limb struck Mr. Bones, all three of the wild dogs drifted to the side and let Jack and Moxie pass by.

Jack kept the limb swinging over his head until he and Moxie were well out into the meadow. It was not as dark in the meadow, but the light was fading there, too. Jack turned back to the trees, and he let the limb swing to a stop. Beside each tree, he saw the shadow of a wild dog like the dark shape of evil.

The wild dogs had never followed Jack into the open meadow. He now felt his fear turning into excitement. He took the limb out of his belt loop, and he flung it at the forest. It hit a tree and dropped to the ground.

"OK, now, Moxie," Jack said. "Now, Moxie—run!"

They turned and began running up through the meadow. Jack grinned with the thrill of another narrow escape. Moxie stayed right next to Jack's pounding feet, and as Jack felt safer, he laughed and whooped and hollered.

"Ha-*ha*!"

Then—and he was almost afraid to do it—Jack looked back over his shoulder, just to make sure, and saw the wild dogs—*all* of the wild dogs—bursting out of the forest.

"Ahhh! Run, Moxie!" Jack screamed. As he sprinted, he kept swinging his empty belt around his head, hoping to confuse the pursuers. He did not look back again. He ran as fast as he could. His leg muscles burned, and the air in his lungs rasped. Then the wild dogs caught up with them. Jack saw them out of the corners of his eyes. They were running and loping along beside them, and Jack expected hard, sharp teeth in his neck.

But they did not attack, and this frightened Jack more. Instead, the wild dogs kept running along on both sides of them, and they were spreading out in a ragged line as they neared the top of the meadow and the flock of sheep.

"Aaaah!" Jack shouted. He had hoped to be saved by the sheep dogs again, but now he needed to warn them. He had hardly any air left in his lungs. "Aaaah! Hey!" he shouted. Jack saw a few sentries come forward. Then the big German shepherd leader dog stepped out in front. Jack wondered what the sheep dogs must be thinking, to see him and little Moxie leading a charge by their enemies, but by this time, they were already there.

Jack was staggering. He was running on fear. He ran right

past the sentry dogs and stumbled into the flock of sheep. He wanted everything possible between him and the wild dogs. He did not turn and look back until he was in the very middle of the flock. Then he crouched down to peer over the backs of the sheep.

Trembling, Jack watched as the sheep panicked and bucked all around him. Beyond the sheep, it looked like the war at the end of the world. The sheep dogs were fighting the wild dogs, and the wild dogs were attacking the sheep. Jack was fighting his fear and getting knocked around by the sheep. He knew he needed to go out and fight the wild dogs, too, but he could not make himself do it.

As they were running through the meadow, Moxie had felt the boy's fear run through her blood, too. It almost made her run faster and leave him behind. But when they reached the front line of sheep dogs—and when the boy dashed into the flock of sheep—Moxie became suddenly charged with new courage. The boy was safer with the sheep, and between Moxie and the fangos were brave Kelso and many more of the courageous sheep dogs. Moxie whirled around, and she snarled at the fangos. She snarled and gnashed her teeth at them savagely. Fear is contagious, as many have said, but Moxie was learning that courage is shared, too.

"Courage!" Kelso yipped. "We are true dogs!"

"True dogs!" the sheep dogs answered.

They leaped again into battle.

Moxie started forward, too, but Kelso called her back.

"Wait," Kelso said. "We must protect Sage."

Moxie followed him as he ran toward the ruins.

40

Then the sheep stampeded, and Jack was knocked down. He took shelter behind a rock as the sheep thundered over him and stormed across the meadow. The wild dog battle rumbled after them. Jack waited a few moments as the snarling and growling faded. Then he lifted his head and stood.

His legs shook badly, and he could not stand long. He sat down on the rock and put his head in his hands.

Jack was alone. Completely alone. He felt beaten. Worse, he felt barely human. He held out his hands and looked at them in the moonlight. *What are these for?* he wondered. *What am I for?* He could almost hear his own thoughts being spoken.

What am I for? he thought again, and so intense was his thinking that this time he did hear his thinking out loud.

Jack put his face into his hands. He heard, *What do I do?*

What do I do? he heard again. He listened to his thought, and it vanished in the air. He needed an answer, but no answer came.

Then he hear another sound. It was the low, ugly sound he had heard too many times—a growing, swelling rumble of growling. It came rumbling across the meadow to him.

What a terrible sound this was—low, evil, and guttural—coming over the meadow from beyond the rock wall. It horrified Jack, but it also made him stand.

Moxie! he thought. Purpose rushed into him, and he began to run toward the sound.

When he got to the ruins, he clambered up onto the old rock wall. What he saw shook him again. It was a dozen or more vicious forest dogs, milling in a semicircle around three sheep dogs.

There was little Moxie standing her ground beside the old blind sheep dog. She held her head low and gnashed her teeth and snarled at the enemy. The big shepherd stood to the other side of the wise old dog. With his huge shoulders and sharp teeth, the shepherd looked fierce enough to hold off the attackers by himself. But there were so many of them, and they moved in whenever the big shepherd turned to look the other way or to check on the old dog beside him.

Jack saw the old dog was in trouble. Thick blood oozed through the matted hair on his neck. The blood shimmered black and silver in the moonlight.

Jack squatted and grabbed a large stone from the top of the wall. It was all he could do to lift it to his shoulder. He squatted again and used his legs to help launch the stone at the snarling pack. But the stone was too heavy. It thudded to the ground and rolled a few feet. The creatures paid the stone no mind. They glanced at Jack with hunger in their eyes and then tightened their arc around the three besieged sheep dogs.

"What do I do?" Jack cried out.

"What do I do?" His lungs and his heart heaved with anguish.

What do I do? screamed the thought in his mind.

Then it happened. As his question echoed inside his brain, it turned into a buzzing that filled his whole body and then his entire being. In Jack's muscles, it became a quivering new strength. On his tongue, it tasted of iron and blood. In his nose, it smelled of blood and memory—of dogs and duty. It filled every sense that Jack had and confused him.

What? Jack thought.

At that moment, the old blind dog raised his shaggy head

off the ground and lifted his nose toward Jack. The old dog looked valiant but helpless.

Jack looked down at him, and in confusion he thought again, *What do I*—

And another's thought answered—*Now you save us.*

Jack put his hands to his ears. "What?"

Now you save us, Jack heard again, but he heard it inside his brain, and he felt it in his entire body. And it was not in his own voice. It was lower, older, and wiser.

Now Jack realized it was the old sheep dog.

The old dog nodded to Jack. *Now you take that walking staff*—

The old dog's mouth had not moved. Jack touched his own lips to make sure it was not he who had spoken.

Then he sensed the old dog's thoughts again. *You get the walking staff, boy*—

Amazing! The thought kept echoing inside Jack's mind—an old, old, wise sound like a bell ringing. Like a bell, the thought echoed throughout Jack's senses.

The staff, the old dog told him. *Fight the fangos with the staff.*

The fangos—yes. Jack was sure he understood it this time. He nodded and he thought, *Yes!*

Jack jumped down from the rock wall, and he dashed through the fangos. One fango lunged and ripped a piece of cloth from his shorts, but Jack ran on, to the corner of the wall, where he thrust his hand in through the bushes. His hand went straight to the staff, and his fingers closed around it. He wrenched it out. Here it was! The hard, heavy weight of it made him feel strong.

Jack turned. As he expected, two fangos were right behind him. They moved as two darker shadows within the black shadow of the wall. Their dim yellow eyes glowed.

Jack lifted the staff above his head, and he spun it in the air.

"*Arrgh—yah!*" he growled. He grabbed the smaller end of the staff, and with both his hands he swung it around him in a great angry circle.

"*Arrgh! Yah!*" He swung it again, and he felt the end of it crack the skull of one fango. The other shadow whimpered and slinked away.

"*Rrragh!*" Jack roared. He leaped over the dead fango and ran back toward the three sheep dogs. He clubbed his way through the whirling, wheeling mob. He got to the dogs' sides. Then he turned and faced the fangos.

"*Rrrragh!*" Jack growled at them. He raised the staff again. "*Rrrrh!*"

The fangos all snarled, but they lowered their heads and cast glances left and right, in sudden indecision.

"*Rrragh!*" Jack roared. The shepherd and Moxie surged forward, adding their strength. And the whole brawling squad of fangos ran.

Jack stood still. He held the staff high, waiting for the fangos to return. They did not come back, and Jack lowered the staff and turned around.

Moxie and the big shepherd dog were gone.

The old sheep dog was still there, lying alone, unmoving. He was a dull and dark pile of matted, bloody fur. The old dog's head lay twisted sideways on the ground.

Where did they go? Jack thought.

Gone to save sheep, the old dog said. *They are vigilant— they are brave—*

But the old dog did not lift his head or move, and Jack saw that he was not breathing.

You are dead, Jack thought.

Dead, the old dog said, in that way that came from within Jack himself. *Dead,* the old dog said. *I am dead but I am here.*

The old dog was dead. And yet he had communicated.

Who are you? Jack thought. *What has happened?*

They call me Sage—I was old—Now I am dead and I will always be old. But I am pleased—Kelso saw you fight—He now knows you are brave—He knows you will help—

Then the whole meaning of everything came to Jack, all at

once. *Then I need to go help,* he thought. He did not say the words aloud, but he could hear himself growling. *I need to help them,* he thought.

Then Sage started chuckling, a kindly old chuckle.

What you need—Sage said—*is what Kelso always says—*

What is that? Jack asked.

Vigilance!

Then Jack felt the hair on the back of his neck stand. A new instinct made him turn.

But Mr. Bones had already leaped.

Jack brought his staff up between them. Mr. Bones hit it and knocked Jack off his feet. Jack rolled onto his back and flipped the fango over him. Jack jumped to his feet and turned. Mr. Bones was already up and facing him. The dread fango snarled. The moon came out again, and the whole scene brightened. The grass was gray. The stones in the grass were white. Mr. Bones was a dull, dark gray-yellow, with his rib cage heaving in the moonlight.

Then the grass rippled as the breeze shifted, and Jack smelled Mr. Bones.

Jack gagged on the odor. He coughed and almost retched. He shook his head to clear it, but it filled again with the stench. It reeked with more than stomach-turning chemistry. It transmitted a whole history of horror and hatred. This was no dog. Mr. Bones was a devil and a traitor. Jack felt his own new dog-senses shudder and recoil as he took in the smell memory of Mr. Bones and his past. It smelled rancid, disloyal, despicable.

Mr. Bones stepped forward. Jack thrust the staff at him, and Mr. Bones grabbed it with his teeth. It was all Jack could do to yank the staff loose. Mr. Bones stepped closer. Jack began to stumble slowly backward, over stones, in a rough half circle, until he was backed against the rock wall. Mr. Bones stepped toward him again and snarled.

B-b-b-b—B-b-b—

Jack did not reply. He swung his staff as hard as he could. The fango ducked it and leaped. But Jack turned behind his staff and swiftly vaulted over the wall. Without looking back, he ran as fast as he could, to the top of the rise, to the top of the sea-cliffs behind his bonfire's woodpile. There, he had room to swing the staff and not trip over a stone. As he waited for Mr. Bones, Jack's hair lifted on the wind. He smelled the salt sea. He heard the waves breaking.

Then Mr. Bones was in front of him, growling.

B-b-b-b—

Jack raised his staff. *One more step, Mr. Bones,* he thought, *and I will bash your brains out.*

Dead dogs don't bite, you know, Jack added with a confident chuckle.

But Mr. Bones stepped forward.

Arrgrh! Jack snarled, and he swung his staff mightily.

Mr. Bones dodged the staff. As it passed him, he leaped. Jack could only get the staff's small end back in between them. The fango hit the staff hard with his throat. His teeth clacked shut, his spew splashed Jack's face, and he fell off to the side. Jack backed away, but Mr. Bones was already up. The fango scrambled around Jack, to keep him pinned against the sea-cliff.

Jack now stood at the very edge of the drop-off. He felt like he might fall, but he also felt like he could fly. Behind and below him, the surf crashed, three hundred feet down. Above him, the wind whipped his hair around his head. In front of him, Mr. Bones crouched low, his breath torn and ragged.

Y-y-yoo—the fango grated.

No, you—Jack growled.

Mr. Bones leaped.

And just as he leaped, Kelso struck him from the side. Jack almost fell backward off the cliff from the surprise. Mr. Bones gave out a shrill snarl, and the two animals rolled along the cliff-top, each clasped in the jaws of the other. They rolled and came apart and hit each other again. This time both were off their front feet, standing up on their back legs. They staggered together for a moment in a twisting embrace. Then Kelso lurched sideways and they toppled off the sea-cliff.

They fell into darkness. Jack could not see their fall. He did not hear anything except the muted crashes of the waves far below him. He stood for a moment and looked out over the dark sea. He saw only the southern stars. He did not see the ship's lantern.

Jack did not see the ship that was now anchored off the island. He was not thinking about ships or civilization or men. He was not thinking in words, as humans do. He was not thinking as dogs think, either, in memories and smells. Jack was not thinking at all. He was feeling alone. He needed something of comfort, some light, some warmth. Some illumination.

In the dark, Jack got down on his hands and knees. He found the tin box and a match, and he lit the woodpile on fire.

41

Moxie was licking her wounds when she saw the glow from the great bonfire. Then she saw the flames themselves reaching up into the sky. She rose to her feet. She was not badly hurt. She wended her way up through the rocks, past dead sheep and dead fangos and a few dead sheep dogs. At the rock wall, Moxie paused by the body of Sage and sensed his spirit.

We are dogs, his spirit said.

We are dogs, Moxie echoed.

She jumped to the top of the wall, into the light.

The fire was blazing enormously now. Bright brands of flame spun up into the sky. The whole hilltop was golden. The waving grass looked molten in the wind. And there, by the fire, at the sea-cliff, stood Jack.

"Moxie!" he called. "Moxie! Come to me." She thrilled at hearing him call her name. She ran to him. Jack knelt and then sat back on the ground. He took Moxie onto his lap and into his arms.

"Moxie," he kept saying. "Moxie."

She understood everything, as Jack told her all that had happened. Wise old Sage had spoken to Jack, and then Fango had attacked him, and then the good, brave Kelso had saved him. But more important for Moxie was that the boy now understood dogs.

And so, in her dog's way, Moxie now told Jack everything—*everything*—and she knew that Jack understood her. Jack was changed. He was wiser and more doglike, but he was still a boy. He was happier and more at ease. He said to her, *I can never leave here, can I?*

No, Moxie told Jack. *You are one of us now.*

The dog and her boy lay down together and curled beside the fire. As the warmth on her face made her head droop, Moxie watched over the boy until he was asleep. She was a dog. She would protect the boy always.

42

In the morning, Jack buried Sage beneath a cross made from the staff. Then he and Moxie walked down through the fango forest. They moved carefully, watchfully, but without the old fear. They knew the fangos were beaten for a while.

They walked out onto the beach and around to the sea-cliffs. Jack wanted to find Kelso, to bury him honorably. Jack felt that he also might benefit from Kelso's spirit, as he had learned from Sage's spirit after Sage had died.

But in the night the tide had come in, and it had gone out, and there was nothing now at all except the wet sand. Moxie sniffed for some telling remnant of brave Kelso. But all of him had gone with the waves.

Jack stood and admired Moxie from the water's edge. He stood ankle deep in the water with his back to the ocean.

Moxie searched and searched, and after a time Jack whistled. Moxie's ears went up, and she came trotting toward him. But she stopped when she got near him. She backed up and growled.

What is it? Jack asked. He looked down around his feet. Then he saw that Moxie was looking behind him.

Jack turned just as a ship's quarterboat crested the surf and slid to a stop on the sand.

The sight of the rowboat made Jack fall down. Behind him, Moxie started barking. Two tattooed men jumped from the boat and came splashing toward Jack. He rolled away from them and started to scramble to his feet, but they had already grabbed him. Jack struggled and he growled. As they lifted him to their shoulders, Jack bit one of them.

"Ow! Hey!" the first sailor barked. "Hey, Jack! I am Toa!"

The sailor looked familiar, but Jack couldn't comprehend him. Jack barked for Moxie.

"And now listen, Tanati! Him like a dog!" the other sailor barked.

They squeezed Jack's arms against his sides.

"Hey, boy-o," growled the first man. "We have you now. Calm!"

Jack barked for Moxie. Moxie barked, *Jack!*

"Ha, ha! He gone dogs, he has," the second man said.

"You been running with dingos?" he asked Jack.

But Jack wouldn't listen. He bit, and the first man yelped and let go of him. Jack twisted himself around, trying to get out of the second man's grasp.

"You! Jack!" the first man shouted.

Jack! Moxie barked.

Moxie!

Now Moxie dashed in at the man's legs, dodging and biting.

"The devil!" The man kicked at Moxie, but he missed and Moxie bit again.

"Damn you, dog!" the man swore.

The other sailor manhandled Jack as he kicked and writhed.

"Him, feisty boy!" he exclaimed. He carried Jack back through the surf foam to the rowboat.

In the rowboat's stern, a third man was waiting. He was a little old man with a white beard and a whalebone pipe. He had one white eyebrow going across both his eyes.

He looked more than familiar, but Jack resisted with fervor.

"Ha, ha! Have it easy with him!" the old sailor barked out.

"Have him easy with *me!* He's a terrier, Cookie!"

"Put a muzzle on him, if needs be," the old man said. "We'll get him aboard ship. I'll feed him. Settle him down. But, now. Hey now! Look at him fight!"

Jack struggled in the rowboat as he watched the first man chase Moxie on the beach. Then the man gave up. He came back to the rowboat, and he shoved the boat's bow around to the surf.

"That little dog is some gumptious," he said, as the other sailor pulled at the oars.

The old sailor said, "She'd have made a good little ship's dog, could we have caught her."

As they rowed away, Moxie harried the waves and she barked and she barked and she barked for Jack.

Jack! Jack! Moxie barked until Jack could no longer hear her. Jack fixed his eyes on the little dog on the beach. *Moxie!* he thought. *Moxie! Wait for me!* And he knew that she had heard him.

But the first sailor pulled at the oars through the swift current. The rowboat moved away from the island, and the image of Moxie got smaller and smaller.

Finally Jack turned his eyes from the island, and now he recognized the old face.

"Yes, it's me," Cookie said. "That's Toa. And Tanati. Captain said we'd come back for you, and here we are. But we'd never have found you if you had not lit that fire."

Jack caught the word *fire*. He held his shirtsleeve to his nose and smelled the fire's smoke. Now the smell memory came back to him, all at once. The fire. The fight. The fango attack. Moxie. Sage. Kelso. *Courage! Vigilance!* Jack relived it in a flash. He jerked himself free and tried to leap out of the boat, but Toa grabbed him and held him down.

Jack should have known he could not outswim Tanati.

As the ship got under sail, Jack had dashed for the gun-wales. He vaulted over the side and plunged into the cold ocean water. But Tanati dove in after Jack and swam beneath him, and he surfaced between Jack and the island. The Maori's tattooed face and pointed teeth made Jack first think he was a seal.

Then Tanati barked like a seal, or so it sounded to Jack. "Jack!" he was saying. "Jack! Jack! Jack! Jackie Tar, boy. You come back!"

But Jack could not listen. He flailed in the water, trying to get around Tanati. But Tanati grabbed him and held him by his hair.

Then, from the ship, Toa hurled a harpoon toward them. It stabbed into the water within arm's reach of Tanati. Tanati grabbed the harpoon's line, and the sailors hauled them back aboard the ship. Toa and Tanati kept laughing and slapping Jack on the back. They were delighted to have found him and not displeased at his wildness. They laughed every time he tried to break away.

"Jack. Jack. Jackie Tar," they kept saying. They had all the ship's men keep repeating his name, as though to remind Jack of who he was.

Later, below decks, Jack sat with a leash on his ankle, tied with one of Cookie's "impossible" knots. Jack was watching Cookie prepare the crew's supper. Cookie worked at the potato scouse with his big ladle, and he worked at Jack with his eyes.

"I missed you, Jack," Cookie was saying. "Without a cabin boy, life is hard."

Life is hard. Life is hard, Jack repeated in his mind. He was beginning to think in words again.

"Life's a challenge, Jack," Cookie was saying. "It's a cry. It's a laugh. Oh, I can tell you some stories."

Then Cookie paused. "And you can tell me some, too."

Cookie nodded, and Jack nodded, too, without really meaning to nod. Then Cookie smiled, and his expression changed around to include many emotions—surprise, consternation, approval, and hope.

And now Jack was smiling, too, and he was meaning to smile. And then he felt his own face changing to match all his emotions. He was laughing. He was crying. He knew he was a boy. He knew that, but it was a terrible strain. His newly learned dog senses were calling him back. He sensed Moxie's devotion, and he vowed to return.

44

Moxie went into Jack's shelter again. She breathed in a full nose's worth of his scent—sweat, smoke, tears, onions, and mutton. With his scent came back the memories, all at once and together, full of barking and laughter and hope. Then Moxie left the shelter and trotted up through the meadow to the top of the sea-cliffs. She sat and panted, and she looked out across the ocean.

From the sea, she kept thinking as she watched the wide water. *Jack will return from the sea.*